the NEW sugar creek gang

The Case of the
Monster in the Creek

Pauline Hutchens Wilson
Sandy Dengler

MOODY PRESS
CHICAGO

Library of Congress Cataloging-in-Publication Data

Wilson, Pauline Hutchens.
    The case of the monster in the creek / Pauline Hutchens
Wilson and Sandy Dengler.
        p.cm. –(New Sugar Creek Gang ; 6)
    Summary: While his sisers babysit their rowdy young
cousins, eleven-year-old Les joins his friends in the New
Sugar Creek Gang as they try to discover what strange
creature is tearing up their favorite park.
    ISBN 0-8024-8666-5
    [1. Parks–Fiction. 2. Babysitting–Fiction. 3. Christian
life–Fiction. 4. Mystery and detective stories.]
I. Dengler, Sandy. II. Title.

PZ7.W69758 Car 2001
[Fic]–dc21

                                                    00-054611

            1 3 5 7 9 10 8 6 4 2

    Printed in the United States of America

INTRODUCTION

I t just isn't the same."

My dad sounded so sad. We stood on the walkway of a freeway overpass, looking out across a sea of new houses. Miles of houses, street after street.

"That line of trees out there is Sugar Creek." He waved an arm toward the hives of condos. "All this used to be farmland. When Paul Hutchens wrote those books about the Sugar Creek Gang, this is the area he wrote about. Right here."

I'm eleven, and, according to Dad, I'm older than most of the *homes* out here. "At least there's still a Sugar Creek," I said. "How far is it from our new place?"

"Couple miles. But the past—that was another world." He looked at me. "I'm sorry the fun is gone."

Dad walked down the slope to our car. I fell in behind him, wishing he didn't feel so sad.

When I was little, he read to me every night. And my favorite books to read were about a bunch of kids called the Sugar Creek Gang. They lived on farms near a creek and had a zillion adventures, mostly out in nature somewhere.

When Dad switched jobs, he found out we were going to move into the very area where the stories took place. He got all excited. I think he expected to find those farms here yet.

He grew up on a farm, so he knows a lot about that stuff. Every few pages, Dad would stop reading and say, "Now, Les, let me tell you about—," and then he'd explain something about spiders or shitepokes or whatever the story was talking about. So good old Les—that's me—learned a lot about farm life and nature when I was little, even though we lived in town.

We drove back to our brand-new home. It was an older house on a shady little back street. Just then it was full of boxes that the moving van had dumped the day before. And I mean full. Not very homey yet, but our beds were put together and made up, so who needs more?

Early next morning, I put on my jacket and found my helmet. It took me a while to dig my bike out of the garageful of jumbled stuff. Then I rode off, headed west.

So Dad thought the fun was gone. I wasn't so sure. That broad strip of trees along the creek looked awfully inviting.

I figured maybe I could find something interesting there. So that's how it all started.

I never guessed that I'd get all wrapped up in a real, true adventure like the ones we'd read about. And I would never *ever* have guessed that the Sugar Creek Gang would come back.

PAULINE HUTCHENS WILSON

1

In an old English legend, the hero Beowulf fought a monster named Grendel and ripped off its arm. Grendel's mom, also a monster, got so mad she almost managed to destroy Beowulf.

"Rowr!" roared Beowulf disarmingly.

That's called a Tom Swiftly—making a pun into an adverb. I learned that in a summer school enrichment class.

But most of what I learned that turned out to be useful later, I learned from the scrapes the Sugar Creek Gang, of which I am part, got into that summer. Not that I wanted to learn those lessons. Some were pretty painful. A few made me just plain angry. And it all had to do with monsters.

My cousin Tyler was really a monster. But he was five, so his sister, Bethany, had him out-monstered. She was two years older, so she had two years' more practice being horrible. Wait until you hear how bad they were.

Then my sisters, Hannah (fourteen) and Catherine (twelve) made a terrible, terrible mistake. They agreed to take care of these two troublemakers for two weeks. Baby-sitting sounded so easy. Not! By the end, we had the cops in on it, plus the gang, a mysterious monstrous destroyer, and a mean old lady in hiking boots.

And it started out so innocently, too.

When I, Les Walker, was eleven, I determined that I would never have kids. I figured I wouldn't mind having a kid like me. I wouldn't mind having kids like my sisters. (Please don't tell them I said so!) But what if I got kids like Tyler and Bethany? I'd go nuts!

Tyler was a screecher. He could shriek loud enough to call in airplanes. He screamed in restaurants. He screamed in church. You didn't dare take him to the library; he'd vibrate the books off the shelf. He thought he owned America. So everyone and everything in America was supposed to do exactly what he wanted.

His sister, Bethany, thought she owned the whole universe. That included her parents and my parents, Tyler, me, everyone in the state, and a couple billion stars. She was a conniver who didn't mind lying. It's the worst kind.

But my sisters, Hannah and Catherine, didn't know this when Auntie Claire called one day. Hannah told the family about the call that night at dinner. At the end, she said, "And, Mom, we're going to do it for half price, since she's our aunt and all."

"I'm very pleased you take family that seriously. Every day for two weeks is a lot of hours."

"We won't have them after five or on weekends, so it's not all that long. We can still have our own life in the evenings."

Catherine shrugged casually. "Besides. What can a couple little kids do?"

Oh, boy.

They arrived Monday morning at seven-thirty. Hannah greeted them at the door with a smile. I ended up hauling in seven cartons of toys. And apparently there were other boxes of toys still at their motel room.

The kids spilled lemonade on the Persian carpet, broke a lamp and the rocking chair—not before they put a huge gouge in the wall from the rocker—made each other cry, and drew blood when one of them kicked Catherine in the shin. That was just the first hour, and the second was like unto it.

Did I run right upstairs and lock my room?

I sure did.

I was headed out to the garage for my bike when Hannah yelled, "Where do you think you're going?"

"Their screaming is rubbing off on you already. To Sugar Creek."

"You're not leaving us alone with these kids!"

"Sure I am. I didn't agree to this arrangement. I'm not part of it at all."

"We'll pay you to stay and help."

"Sorry. I'm too young to legally baby-sit." And I left.

Yesterday, Tiny had e-mailed everyone, setting up a meeting of the Sugar Creek Gang. We always got together in the picnic area at the front of Sugar Creek County Park on the other side of town.

Tiny and Mike were there when I arrived.

Tiny (his name is Clarence Wilson, but he tries not to tell people that) sat on a picnic table—yes, I mean on the table, with his feet on the seat. He had his binoculars out, watching birds in the trees along the creek. But then, he almost always had his binoculars with him. I sometimes wondered if he wore them around his neck in church. He was the tallest, the oldest by a few months, and the skinniest of the Sugar Creek Gang. Now Lynn and I were thin, but he was a scarecrow. He was also black, and thoughtless people sometimes asked him how he liked basketball. He hated basketball.

Mike Alvarado was only ten and small for his size, so he and Tiny looked kind of goofy together. But friendship is what counts. Mike was stronger than any two of us. If you wanted a hippo picked up or a big lawnmower, he was your man.

I was redheaded and freckled; I looked goofy with or without companions.

Bits (Elizabeth, to her teachers) Ware came rolling in a few minutes later. I once said that her ponytail was mousy brown. I wouldn't say that again for a million bucks. She was as strong as I was.

Lynn Wing, Japanese-Chinese and quiet as a mouse in a box of tissue, arrived last. She had an oversized violin case on her back. "Sorry I'm late. Music lesson ran over."

Tiny looked from face to face. "The reason I called this meeting—no, there's two reasons.

One reason is, I'm bored. But the other one is more important. I walked along the swamp trail yesterday, and I couldn't believe all the damage I saw. Somebody is really tearing up Sugar Creek."

2

L et's go check it out!" I was always ready to go through the park. I couldn't believe someone would deliberately tear anything up, but you never know. So we all tooled our bikes back up the trail.

Sugar Creek County Park ran for a couple of miles along Sugar Creek. Its chainlink fence enclosed woods and some open glades for maybe a quarter of a mile on either side of the stream. It was a kind of urban wilderness. Once you started back in the trails, the trees and bushes closed in around you. They smothered the civilization outside the fence so that you didn't notice it. They turned the sunlight into scattered, dancing spots.

Everything lived there: deer sometimes, raccoons and possums all the time, and all kinds of birds. Frogs hid along the shore until just before you got there, then jumped into the creek. Turtles and snakes sunned themselves near the water or swam around in it with hardly a ripple.

We took the Swamp Loop, a side trail that led around to where we often ate lunch. There, you sat on the grassy riverbank while Mother Nature popped surprises at you. It might be a kingfisher grabbing a minnow, or it might be a heron. Out in the middle, turtles clustered on top of a log.

But here on the shore, Tiny pointed out, someone had been pulling up the cattails and tall grasses.

"Look!" Lynn pointed. "They even ripped up some wild iris. Who would do a thing like that? The iris is so beautiful in the spring."

Tiny looked grim. "Like someone just grabbed handfuls and yanked."

Mike studied the damage. "I don't know 'bout iris, but cattails are good to eat. Maybe somebody was harvesting, y'know? Somebody who doesn't have much and figured it's a free meal. See? Some of them look cut."

"Ought to be more careful about pulling up the other stuff, if that's what it is." Tiny did not take kindly to anyone who messed up nature.

We hung around the park another hour or two, exploring. There were a couple other places where streamside plants were torn up. In side pools where the current didn't flow, long, grassy leaves and things floated on the surface.

Mike is a good tracker, so we had an expert on the job. He couldn't find any clear tracks, just traces. We figured that any tracks had been washed out by the heavy rain last night.

We got so wrapped up in the puzzle that I forgot all about the two little monsters until we started home again. Would the house still be standing when I rode up my street?

It was. That was a relief.

I dumped my bike and went inside and on into the kitchen. "Hi, Mom. What's for lunch?"

"Sandwiches and soup, the same as usual."

"Good. I'm hungry, the same as usual."

I washed up and sat down at the table. I told her about the destruction at the park. I mentioned that we couldn't think of anyone who would do that.

Mom said, "I can think of two. Your sisters are baby-sitting them. The girls are at their wits' end, and it's only halfway through the first day."

"Hannah and Catherine are good soldiers, Mom. The brats caught them by surprise is all. I'll bet anything Hannah has everything organized by tomorrow, and they'll be ready for them. Not even those two kids are a match for Hannah and Catherine when they're fighting a war."

Mom laughed. "You mean they'll develop a military strategy?"

"Or pool their money and buy a big anchor to chain the kids to. I forget—why is Auntie Claire in town?"

"She's working on a research project at the university. Her former professor asked her to help. They'll be able to write at least one and maybe two important papers out of it."

"That's good, huh?"

"That's good." Mom set a big soup tureen on the table. "Pour the milk, please."

I headed for the fridge. "Where is she staying?"

"Easyrest Motel on Fourth. She and the children got in late yesterday evening. We talked on the phone, but I haven't been over there yet. She says they have a very nice suite with a separate bedroom."

"Uncle Rob didn't come, I guess." I set the milk out and went to the cupboard for the glasses.

"He had to stay home and work."

Upstairs, something crashed. I mean really crashed.

"Smart man," I opined.

How my sisters made it through the rest of the day I don't know because I went over to Bits's to play video games. I won three out of five this time, which is a clear majority, for once. I admit that most of the other times, she'd won.

Auntie Claire came at a few minutes after five and retrieved her little darlings. Hannah and Catherine smiled sweetly and waved goodbye.

The door closed.

"I can't believe it!" Hannah roared. "Those are the most undisciplined little criminals in the universe!"

So I explained my theory that Tyler thought America belonged to him and Bethany thought the universe belonged to her.

"You got that right!" Hannah popped a soft drink before dinner, and Mom didn't say a word. (Mom usually frowned on that, but she must have taken a lot of pity on the girls.) "Only Bethany is always trying to grab America away from Tyler so she can own that, too. They fight constantly!"

"Yeah," Catherine agreed. She opened a soda as well, without getting yelled at. "Auntie Claire doesn't believe in punishment. We're just supposed to show them what they're doing wrong, and then, naturally, they won't do it anymore. What baloney!"

"Where did she get that notion, Mom?" Hannah asked. "You and Dad are as strict as prison wardens."

"I don't know." Mom pulled a tray of oven-fried chicken out of the oven. "Your Aunt Claire is two years younger than I, and she tended to resent it a lot more when we were disciplined. She usually got yelled at more, too. Possibly she's trying to be different than our parents were, but it seems she's a little too different."

"That's a true story!" Catherine put out the flatware. That was her job this week. "She made us agree to no spanking. No angry words. I can't believe she'd think that works. We're not even allowed to yell at them."

"So how come you're allowed to yell at me?" I demanded. "You might warp me, and I'll be ruined forever. You never know."

"Hardly." Hannah blipped my nose with her finger. "At least when we yell at you, little bro, you know we did it. These two monsters don't even hear us."

3

The second day of my sisters' battle with monsters promised to be better.

Hannah announced at breakfast, "We figured out how to handle this. Divide and conquer. We entertain Bethany in one room and Tyler in another, and then we switch off. When they're apart, they won't think of so much ugly stuff to do."

"What'd I tell you, Mom?" I smugly dug into my cereal.

Hannah glared at me. "What does that mean?"

"Superior military tactics," I replied.

But Mom filled her in.

Dad came down for breakfast and hinted broadly that the grass ought to be a lot shorter.

Now this was not small talk. I received an allowance, like most kids. And I was expected to do certain chores. The allowance and the chores were not directly related. I mean, the allowance came, regardless. And if I didn't get any money, the chores were still mine to do anyway. However—and it's a big however—however, if I did chores without being asked, I got extra. It didn't take a rocket scientist to figure out that it paid to listen to hints.

So after breakfast I got out the mower and

the electric trimmer. I had gassed up the mower and was all set to yank the cord and touch it off when Bits came rolling in at a hundred miles an hour.

"Les! I almost got eaten up by a monster in Sugar Creek!"

"You want to talk about monsters? Let me tell you about Tyler and Bethany."

She was instantly furious. She's very good at getting furious instantly. "You don't believe me!"

"Bits. How many years have you spent messing around Sugar Creek? And in that time, how many monsters have you seen, total?"

"One! This morning. It's real, Les! It came after me from under the water. I just missed being grabbed. It was this big!" And she held her hands as wide apart as she could get them.

"You should tell Tiny. He's the one who might have a clue what it is."

And she turned cold. That's the only way I can describe it. "I did. I called him up. He doesn't believe me, either."

"I didn't say I didn't believe you."

"It's plain enough." She chewed on me for a while, but I won't write it all down. Then she finished with, "Why would I lie about something like that? You are so dense, Les. You all are!" She paused. "Well? Are you coming with me to go see?"

"I want to finish up the yard before it gets too hot."

So she chewed on me some more, picked

up her bike, and went home—which was right across the street, incidentally.

Mowing the lawn at our house was more than just shoving the mower around without missing spots. You gassed the mower and checked the oil. When you were done, you cleaned it up. That meant clawing out all the mushed grass around the walls inside where the blade turned (and you always take the top wire off the spark plug first, so it can't cough and compression start if the blade is turned. Just one fast spin of the blade can take a finger off). It also meant wiping it off. Finally, you put the mower away properly in its parking space in the shed.

The trimming went fast. You didn't have to do nearly as much to an electric trimmer. Coil the cord and hang it up; that was about all.

And all the while I was working, I was thinking. Bits was a down-to-earth person, not given to lying. So she was right: Why would she lie, and especially, why would she make up a lie that was so preposterous? A monster lurking in Sugar Creek was really far-fetched. If you want to get away with a bald-faced lie, make it believable.

On the other hand, Tiny didn't believe her, either.

So after lunch—and I ate early to miss the rush of sisters and monsters—I put on my helmet and rode over to Sugar Creek.

Someone once wrote a song about the hazy, lazy days of summer. That's Sugar Creek on a summer afternoon. I chained up the bike at the rack and walked from the sun into cathedral quiet shade.

The woods lost their sharp edges and got hazy in the heat. The heat itself lost its intensity. The woods were cool and dark and mellow. They didn't just look hazy; they *felt* hazy.

The birds must have been busy doing other things, because they didn't sing much. They didn't even twitter much. Everything had dropped to a sort of casual, easygoing "don't worry, be happy" mood.

I felt that way, too, as I walked the dirt paths. Monsters? Not in this great weather.

When Bits was roaring along in her super snit, I didn't get to ask her where she had been when the monster attacked. And later, I forgot to ask. But most of us Creekers, when we visited the park, started out at our favorite place on the Swamp Loop. She'd come to my house fairly early, which means she probably didn't get very far back into the park. So I'd start at our favorite place.

Now understand, this is not to mean that I believed her. It was more a "what if" than a definite "she saw it."

I did see fresh bike tracks, so she probably was here.

I didn't get very far along the Swamp Loop, though, because a monster attacked *me*.

It wasn't Bits's monster down in the water. This monster was a really cranky, frightening old woman. I don't know how old. Once they're over thirty, I can't tell. She wore canvas shorts and bulky, thick-soled hiking boots. Her hair was straight, short, and gray. She carried a long walking stick that looked like something you didn't want to get too close to. Mostly, she seemed she ought to be up in the Alps yodeling.

"You!" she roared and pointed at me. "Get out!"

My highly intelligent answer was, "Huh?"

"You destructive little ruffians stay out of this park! All you do is tear it up! You kill the ducks and animals! And don't you ever let me catch you in here again!" She raised her walking stick.

I think I remembered to say, "Yes, ma'am!" but don't bet on it. What you can bet on is that I turned tail and ran.

4

Dinner. No matter how weird or rotten the day went, there was always dinner. Dinner was late because Dad was late. But then, Auntie Claire was going to be late picking up her little land mines this evening. Were my sisters in a fury, or what?

Finally we settled at the table, and Mom set out her big casserole with world-class beef stroganoff in it. You scooped noodles onto your plate, then spooned stroganoff on top of them. Nothing better. And of course, we discussed the world as we ate.

Hannah and Catherine went on at length about their terrible day. Great length. Great, great length. Apparently dividing and conquering didn't work. The kids thought up just as much mischief individually as they did as a matched set. After my poor sisters' horrid tale, mine seemed pretty tame.

However, I got my chance to describe Bits's story and my encounter with the woman in the park. I ended with, "She can't really keep us out, can she, Dad? I mean, the Gang? She said 'ruffians.' More than one."

"No. It's a public park. She was out of bounds even if you had been doing something destructive. I trust you weren't." He glanced sideways at me.

"No, sir."

He nodded. "If you were, it would take a police officer to evict you anyway. But thank you for not arguing with her. Let adults do the arguing."

Mom asked, "What do you think the monster is?"

"I don't know. Imagination, maybe. But I didn't think Bits had that much imagination. Lynn, yes. Mike, yes. Bits, no."

But enough about my troubles. Hannah and Catherine had caught their breath, and they were bored with my tame little monsters who only attacked people. So we heard round two of their day. I excused myself, took my plate to the sink, and headed out the door.

"Where are you going?" Mom interrupted her daughters' litany of woe.

"Up to Lynn's. See if she has any ideas."

"Be back by dark."

"Yes, ma'am."

I walked to Lynn's. It's only four doors up the street. As I approached her house, though, I heard a horrible monster shrieking. It went up the scale note by note, then down. But calling them "notes" suggests they were music. Uh-uh. They were wailing.

I was almost afraid to knock on the door.

Mrs. Wing answered. She was a pleasant lady, not much taller than I but much more graceful. From her appearance, you'd sort of expect to hear a Japanese accent. She didn't have any. "Born and bred in the USA," she was always proud to say.

"Well, Les! Good evening. Come on in. Lynn is upstairs practicing."

"Practicing what, exactly?"

"Her instrument."

There are instruments of music and instruments of torture. I was afraid to ask which one this was.

As I climbed the carpeted stairs, the wailing changed pitch and went up and down a different scale.

The Wings had a music room. Probably it had started out in life as a front bedroom. But they had converted it to other uses. A piano sat in one corner, and a sewing machine in the other. So it was a room of more than one purpose.

In the middle, Lynn sat on a chair before a music stand, watching the page intently as she sawed on a fiddle.

She glanced up at me. "Hi, Les."

"I didn't know you played the violin." I was really stretching the term *play*.

She quit playing and put her bow and instrument of torture in her lap. "You did too. And it's not a violin. It's a viola. It's bigger than a violin, and the strings are a little different. It can't go up as high as a violin, but it can go lower. It's in the middle between the violin and the cello."

That was a lot more than I really wanted to

know. "Now that I look, yeah, it seems bigger than a fiddle."

"You see," Lynn said in that quiet voice, "there are all sorts of people who play the violin. They're what they call the stars of the orchestra. But not many people are violists. Orchestras usually need violas. I never want to be a soloist or a concertmaster or anything, so this is perfect for me."

"What orchestra hires an eleven-year-old girl?"

"Regional junior orchestra. They audition in fall. I probably won't make it this year, but next year I have a chance."

With a LOT of work, I thought. Out loud, I explained about Bits's claim. I said that Tiny didn't believe her. And I told Lynn about the old woman.

She studied the floor a few moments. "The old lady accused you of killing ducks?"

"Yeah. And I'm not sure I would call her a lady."

She smiled briefly. "Do you know if they were shot, or what?"

"She didn't say. I didn't go back down the trail, so I wouldn't know what she saw that would look like dead ducks."

"That's so strange."

We batted ideas back and forth for a few minutes, but we didn't come up with anything. The key seemed to be Tiny. If anyone would have a good guess, it would be Tiny.

I didn't want to go home. I wanted to go

anywhere except home. The old woman had pretty much killed my desire to go prowling around Sugar Creek, too. That left the library. But then I'd have to stop by the house to get my bike, and what if my sisters collared me for guard duty? I didn't have a pit bull or something to help control those two kids with.

I stood up. "Well, see you. Sorry to bother you."

"No bother. Say, are you taking violin lessons?"

"No," I replied. "Why would you ask *that*?"

"Well, once in a while I hear this sort of muffled screech from down toward your place, as if you scraped your bow across a violin wrong. Very high-pitched."

"Oh. I'll bet that's Tyler."

"Tyler takes violin? Who's Tyler?"

Hey. She asked. So I gave her a sort of short summary of my cousins. Even though I trimmed it down to hit only the highlights, it took another half hour.

5

Dad shelved his books very neatly by topic. Fiction here, travel there, law up there. One whole wall of his office was nothing but bookshelves.

Mom shelved hers by subject, too, mostly school texts and papers. I don't think she bothered sorting cookbooks, though.

Me? I shelved mine by size. My bookshelf spaces were different heights. So I put all the huge books on the shelf that had lots of headroom, and all my really little books, like Golden Nature Guides and such, were on the low, narrow shelf. And up on the very top, I stacked my maps.

I loved maps. And my most favorite map was a copy of one drawn a couple years before Columbus made his voyage to India and accidentally bumped into this continent that no one knew anything about yet.

It was in English, sort of. The spelling was weird, but, spelling aside, the map was fantastic.

The Mediterranean was about where it ought to be, and the cartographer—that's what we map lovers call a mapmaker—got the shape of Europe right. And North Africa. And even some of Asia. But out in the Atlantic, where

North and South America lay hidden and unknown, the mapmaker drew monsters.

They coiled like snakes, loop after loop arching out of boiling water. They stuck fearsome heads up out of the billows, mouths wide open, just waiting for some foolish ship to get close enough. There was another monster in the lower right, down where the Indian Ocean really is. It didn't look too bad until you realized it had a little ship in its teeth—and the ship was buckling in half. So apparently you weren't going to fall off the end of the flat earth after all. A monster would eat you first.

After I returned from Lynn's, I locked myself in my room and pulled that map down off the shelf. I laid it out and looked at the monsters awhile. I absorbed their details—the scales, the nostrils. Who could think up such things? Could Bits? No.

Something was in Sugar Creek. The thought echoed over and over.

A heavy body—or something—thumped against my door so loudly I jumped a foot straight up. The doorknob rattled.

"Let me in!" screamed Tyler.

"No. Too much stuff in here that can get broken."

"I won't break anything." Even when he talked normally, he shouted.

"What about Hannah's light? And Catherine's CD player?"

"That was an accident. Let me in."

"No. Too many *potential* accidents." And I

was very proud of myself for working the word "potential" into a conversation. It was a spelling-and-vocabulary word in my advanced English class last year. Most of the words we learned there we never saw again.

He alternately screamed and pounded on the door, and I ignored him. I thought any minute that a little shoe was going to come smashing through the door panel. But it's an old house with strong oak doors.

Something was in Sugar Creek.

I got out my mammal book and paged through the drawings in the middle. I didn't see anything that lived on or near the water that would be big enough to scare Bits like that. Bits is not one who scares.

Something big was in Sugar Creek. It ripped up plants and attacked people.

Bits had to be imagining things.

What was I going to do next? It was either leave the room—and old Leather-lungs was still banging away on the other side of the door—or explore monsters. I chose to explore. Do you blame me?

The old King James version of the Bible had some monsters in it. I'd learned that when the translators back around 1600 came upon some words for animals, they didn't know what they were. They were all Englishmen who had never lived in the lands of the Bible. The original Bible writers, the Jews, knew what they were talking about, of course. But the Englishmen had no idea what kinds of animals lived in the

Holy Land. In fact, many of the animals that lived there when the Old Testament was written had died out by 1600. There were no lions left, for instance.

So what was that animal mentioned in Isaiah 14:29 or Jeremiah 8:17? They had no idea. It was fearsome and dangerous. It was deadly. The best they could come up with was "cockatrice." That is supposed to be a rooster with a snake's tail. If you look at it, or it looks at you, you're dead.

Oh yeah, sure, we say today. But back then, people believed there were such things. The Englishmen had never seen a cockatrice. But they figured such things might still exist in far away places—in Bible lands, for instance.

Nowadays, we know something that the translators didn't: that old Hebrew word means *adder,* a poisonous snake like a rattlesnake but no rattle.

And that got me thinking. I was pretty sure Bits wasn't just making anything up. What if that something in Sugar Creek couldn't be identified because it was something that had never been seen before? What if it was a complete unknown, like the King James people's adder? It lived somewhere but had never been seen here before. Or maybe it was like those monsters out in the oceans on my map—an imaginary something based on a real something that was actually very different.

My breastbone tickled!

Could something live in Sugar Creek without anyone ever seeing it at least once? I couldn't believe that. But on the other hand, stranger things had happened. Maybe it just never showed itself before. Or maybe this was the first time it attacked. Or maybe it wasn't the first time it attacked, but the earlier attacks were successful and the people who saw it just disappeared. In other words, maybe Bits was the first one to get away alive.

How would we go about revealing such a monster to the world? First we'd have to catch one—or kill it. No, Lynn would have a conniption if we even mentioned killing it. Maybe Tiny would, too. So we'd have to catch it.

I thought about the big picture that would be in the paper—of the Sugar Creek Gang standing around the cage with this monster in it. The article would tell how we discovered it. And the article would probably get some of the facts wrong. Dad claimed that they always did. But so what? There would be that picture.

Only one big question remained to be answered. How in the world do you catch an unknown monster?

6

Bits's dad was a police officer, but he couldn't be everywhere at once.

He wasn't there, for instance, when the cops arrested Tiny.

I heard about it later, because Tiny told us all about it. Tiny sent e-mail messages around as soon as he got home from his brush with the law. We met the next morning at the picnic table, as usual.

Tiny explained it this way: It started when Bits convinced Tiny that he ought to go back into Sugar Creek Park and try to get a look at the monster she was dead certain was there.

So he did. He said he never noticed the woman in hiking boots or saw her along any of the trails. But apparently she saw him. She called the cops on her cell phone. They came out and got him while he was working his way along the creek bank.

Actually, I guess they didn't arrest him. Not exactly. They detained him and kicked him out of the park and told him not to go back there.

"What were you doing that she thought was so awful?" I asked.

"Nothing!" Tiny protested. "I was looking for tracks along the shore. I figured if something that size is out there, it's going to make marks that you can see in the mud. Don't you think?"

"Sounds right." And I told them my theory about an unknown monster.

Tiny wrinkled his nose. "Nah. I doubt it. I don't know anything that would meet the requirements."

"Exactly! Nobody knows about it. That's the whole point. That's what 'unknown' means!"

Bits fumed. "I wish my dad had been there. He'd set the cops straight. If Tiny wasn't doing anything, they didn't have probable cause to kick him out!"

"What's 'probable cause'?" I asked.

"It just means they have to have some clear reason to lean on him. Dad told me about it once."

"When it comes to leaning on someone," Tiny said gloomily, "it helps to be carrying some weight. And the cops, man, they have all the weight."

"I'll ask Dad tonight about what we can do," I said. "Since he's a lawyer, he knows what he would say if he was defending you in court. So he'll know what you can and can't do. If we want to find the monster in the creek, we need you with us."

Tiny wagged his head. "So you're still sure there's something down there that nobody's ever seen."

"*I* saw it!" Bits snapped. "And it's very nice, thank you, to find at least one other person who believes me."

"Two others. I believe you," Lynn added in her quiet voice. "You don't lie."

"But it's prepoceros!" Mike exclaimed, mixing up preposterous with rhinoceros.

And that's the way the conversation went for the next half hour. I kept trying to get them enthusiastic about chasing monsters or at least willing to consider it. All they wanted to talk about was the wrong done to Tiny. And of course, talking it to death, over and over, wasn't going to do a solitary thing. As nearly as I could tell, the meeting ended with everyone frustrated. I know I was, because we weren't making any plans to go catch a monster.

When I got home for lunch, Mom was off to a meeting and my sisters were reduced to quivering little blobs of jelly. Apparently, not only did plan B of their military tactics fail miserably, so did their backup plan. And that plan, C, was the only thing they had left. I think that when they took the job, they had envisioned a cakewalk. They were getting a death march.

As I was finishing my lunch, Hannah said pointedly, "Les? Wouldn't you and Tyler like to go for a walk?"

Tyler and I both replied, "No." He didn't like the idea any better than I did.

"Les." Hannah's voice took on a sharp edge —a very sharp edge. "I think it would be great if you and Tyler went out for a while and, you know, bonded."

"Hey, Tyler. You want to bond?" I asked him.

"No! I want to chop wood again, like we did yesterday."

I frowned at my sisters. "You got him cutting wood? But we don't have a wood stove."

"We went down to the living history exhibitions at the museum," Catherine explained. "The guide let him and some other kids try to chop wood. He almost killed three people. They barely got the hatchet away from him in time."

"Catherine," Hannah chided, "you're always exaggerating. He didn't almost kill three people. But I admit he could have maimed them."

"I don't want to bond, and I don't want to bleed. No. End of consideration." I picked up my plate and headed for the kitchen sink.

Bethany was apparently done, too, since she bobbed up out of her chair and headed for the stairs.

"Bethany!" I called. "Come and carry your plate and glass to the sink."

"You can't make me!" And up the stairs she went.

"Catherine." Hannah nodded toward the stairs.

"It's your turn!" Catherine whined.

"Go! And hurry!"

And so Catherine left half her soup and some sandwich still uneaten and beat it upstairs to keep Bethany from ripping the second story off the house.

Hannah whispered hoarsely, "Les, sit down. How much do you want?"

I sat down beside her. "You don't have enough money. Not even Mom and Dad have enough money to bribe me into doing your baby-sitting for you."

"Les, name a price."

"Priceless. I'm not getting near that can of worms."

"Les, please. Just this afternoon. Please."

I guess it was her tone of voice that got me. Hannah could be demanding at times. She could whine. She could wheedle. She could so frequently be infuriating. But this tone of voice was something new. This time she was desperate. More than desperate. At wits' end. The girl was in genuine, obvious pain.

"Please, Les," she whispered.

I looked at Tyler. He was scarfing down the last of his soup. "I'm going to hate myself for this. OK. I guess. What do you want me to do with him?"

The look of relief on her face was pitiful to see. "I don't care. Anything you want. Take him for a walk. Wear him down. Lock him in a closet. Just take him for a few hours."

I thought about this a few moments. "Sugar Creek is too far away on foot, and I don't want to put him on my bike. How about Merrymount?"

"Perfect! But be careful on Oakdale Boulevard. He has a tendency to forget and run out into the street."

I assumed this was the voice of experience speaking. So I agreed. "You want me to wear him down, so we'll stay off Oakdale and take side streets over. You know. Little streets. No traffic but the long way around."

"That'd be great." She laid a hand on my arm. "Thank you, Les. You don't know how grateful I am."

I watched Tyler drop a cracker on the floor deliberately and then stomp on it. This was obviously going to be a situation requiring lots of prayer as well as patience. "I think I'm about to find out."

7

I have always had a good, healthy fear of yo-yos ever since I tried to operate one and it whipped back around and bopped me right square in the nose. It gave me a bloody nose and everything. After that, I would let other people be the yo-yo experts, and walk the dog or do some other yo-yo trick. I stuck to toys that don't bite back. When you're clumsy and a kid, there aren't many of them.

Maybe that's what bothered me so much about Tyler. He was a yo-yo. He was constantly moving, pulsing in and out, tugging at the string, circling me. He could not simply walk like a normal human being. It was usually a dead run, and it was always in unexpected directions.

"Yes, Les," you might say, "but he wouldn't give you a bloody nose."

"You want to bet?" would be my reply.

A yo-yo isn't supposed to, either, but it did.

Tyler almost did, also. Over by Peach Street, a dead branch had fallen off a tree. He grabbed it and started swinging it around, yelling. Of course, he didn't just put it down because I told him to. I had to wrestle it away. And he very nearly corked me as I was trying to get it away from him.

That is why I grabbed him by the wrist and held his arm as we crossed Oakdale, the only busy street on the roundabout way I was taking him. I couldn't trust him to simply cross the street the way he was supposed to.

It was more roundabout than I intended, though. I got lost on dead ends a couple of times. I knew in general where the park was, and I knew where we lived. I knew Oakdale was the street to take if you wanted to simply get there. The rest was "bluff and grin."

Merrymount Park was one of those city parks that was mostly a couple acres of lawn. It held playground stuff for real little kids, swings and teeter-totters for medium-sized kids, a wooden jungle gym to climb on, a softball diamond in one corner, and a soccer field in another. In the middle was a fair-sized duck pond. It filled to the brim in rainy weather and shrank down to a sort of mud hole in very dry weather. But any time of year you had half a dozen ducks on it.

The ducks weren't always actually on it. Sometimes they just hung around near it. They napped on the grassy bank, heads tucked back under their wings. They loafed, bobbing off-shore. Or they walked around gurgling deep in their snaky throats, begging popcorn and potato chips off the park's visitors. But it was their home all year. They were four brownish ducks, a big white one with a goofy blue-and-purple featherless head (which was, I understand, either

Muscovy or part Muscovy), and a pair of tame mallards.

When Tyler and I arrived, we had the whole park to ourselves. He headed straight as an arrow for the ducks, of course. They were snoozing up on the bank. He came at them yelling and waving his arms. They woke up instantly and plunged into the water, splashing like crazy.

A mallard shook himself, ruffling his feathers, as he floated. He had a "What in the wide world was that!" look on his face.

I yelled at Tyler to leave the ducks alone. Tyler ignored me. He ran around the shore trying to reach them. But they were savvy about little kids and stayed well out on the water. Then Tyler ran off around to the far side.

I knew that a cyclone fence surrounded the park, so he couldn't run away. I knew a gravel parking lot filled the area near the fence where he was going. So I sat down on a picnic bench beside the pond and gathered my strength, certain that I would soon need it.

Presently, Tyler came running back toward the pond. The ducks were still out in the middle, cruising in circles where he couldn't reach them, so I wasn't worried.

I should have been.

Up in the parking area, he had been gathering stones! Now he stood on the shore opposite where I was. He started pegging rocks at the ducks. For a kindergartener, he could throw like you wouldn't believe. Before I could jump to my feet and get around the pond to stop him, he had bopped the baldheaded Muscovy.

I managed to wrench the stones out of his hands and toss them into the pond—not near the ducks!

Disgusted, I dragged him over to the play equipment. "Here. Wear yourself out. Hold your breath until your face turns blue. I don't care. Just quit getting into trouble."

"Push me on the swing."

"You can push yourself." But I ended up pushing him anyway. It was easier than saying, "Do it yourself," a hundred times. He sure could wear you out by repeating something constantly.

That lasted three minutes. He jumped off the swing and almost broke an ankle. Then he was away to the slide. He slid down once and tried to climb up the slide part. That's a no-no in any of the city's parks and school playgrounds. Yelling at him did no good. He got to the top, slid down, and was starting back up when I grabbed him around the waist and pulled him off the board.

I prayed that I would be patient. After all, this was only a five-year-old kid.

He ran right to the teeter-totter and demanded that I teeter him.

"I'm too heavy for you."

"Teeter me!"

I weighed a lot more than he, of course. So I ended up standing by my end of the seesaw and moving it up and down with my arms and hands. Boy, that sure wears you out in a hurry. But it bored him in a minute, and he was off the seesaw and gone to the merry-go-round.

By now, we were no longer alone. A little girl of three or four had arrived with her mom. She was on the merry-go-round while her mom turned it by hand. Tyler grabbed a handhold and started running, making the merry-go-round go around much faster than it ought. Not merry at all.

The little girl started crying, and her mom got mad. I don't blame either one of them.

I heard once that, when you pray for patience, God will give you something to try your patience and in that way strengthen it. I was beginning to discover you get what you ask for, but not the easy way.

I couldn't snatch Tyler away safely, so I grabbed a merry-go-round rail and dragged the whole thing to a halt. It just about ripped my shoes off.

Tyler shrieked and fought me. I held firm.

The little girl was headed now for one of those ponies that perch on a big spring. It bobs back and forth when you get it going.

Tyler ran ahead of her and grabbed the pony. He hauled himself aboard, much too big for the thing. He got it swinging back and forth.

When the little girl ran toward the swings, he bailed off the pony. He saw which swing she was aimed at and got to it before she did. He plopped into it and started swinging, just about knocking her over.

I was so mad I didn't care anymore. If I spilled him and he broke both legs and a tooth or two, it would serve him right! I managed to catch one chain and get him stopped. I dragged him off and looked to see where the little girl was going. This time I'd get to him in time to stop him.

But he fooled me by heading back for the ducks again. The ducks were just now coming ashore, settling down after his first attack on them. He ran right for them, and the swings were close enough to the pond that he managed to scatter the flock. They ran in all directions, squawking. Feathers flew. He turned on the female mallard, who was cut off from the rest of them. She took to the air, flapping desperately, and circled low to reach the pond.

Tyler made a wild lunge to catch the duck in midair. But he lost his balance. In a tangle of legs and flapping arms, he rolled down the slippery mud bank and splashed right into the pond.

8

I pumped my fist in the air. "Yes!"

I knew that gloating wasn't the Christian thing to do. And I knew I was supposed to be keeping this sweet, charming little boy from coming to harm. But, oh, how I loved seeing him roll into the drink! That really, really made my day.

Now here's a tip if you ever watch small kids: little children can drown in a couple inches of water. They slip, it covers their faces, and they get confused about how to get out. They take a deep breath, and that's it. A little child can drown in a bathtub of water so shallow that the back of his head is still dry. You must never leave a little kid alone in a bathtub for even a minute. Never.

Or in a duck pond.

The water there was very shallow along the edge, but Tyler's face went under anyway. So I was ready to grab him if he didn't pop up by himself right away.

He did, though. He came up hacking and coughing and shrieking, in equal parts. He sat in the mud and water and howled, no doubt expecting me to come running. I stood on the shore and waited.

He shrieked louder.

I yelled back, "It serves you right. You were a jerk. You don't chase the ducks!"

And that really made him mad!

But finally he crawled out, slipping and sliding, and stood up. I clamped his wrist in a death grip. He dripped, totally soaked. And he dripped not just water but mud as well.

"Time to go home."

He tried to yank away, but I had him in a grasp of iron. We headed for the gate, homeward bound.

"Let loose of me!" He struggled.

"No."

"Yes!"

"No." One of the reasons I held him like that was so he wouldn't smear himself all over me. What a royal mess he was. But I sure wasn't going to tell him that, or he'd get me all wet and muddy on purpose. If I was going to get wet and muddy, I wanted it to be because I was doing something fun. This was definitely not fun.

We left the park and walked back the side streets toward home, looping around the long way but by a different route from the one we took when coming.

Finally he quit fighting me so much, and I could let go.

"Why did you call me a jerk?" he yelled. He always yelled everything he said.

"Because that's what you were."

"Then why did you take me to the park?"

"As a favor to my sisters."

He stared at me. "You lie! You wouldn't do a favor for your sisters."

"I don't lie."

"You'd really do a favor for your sisters?"

He made it sound like the freakiest idea ever thought of. And I understood why. To him, "sister" meant Bethany. She was the only sister he'd known in his five years. He could not imagine doing anything nice for his sister, not in a million years. He and Bethany were dog and cat. So no wonder he was amazed.

And I also realized then that, much as I complained about them, Catherine and Hannah were not all that bad. In fact, they were pretty good. Sure, I would continue to grumble about them. After all, it was my job as a little brother to complain. But I decided to be a lot more forgiving. When I forgot to, all I'd have to think about would be, *You know, Les, they could be like Bethany.*

And on the other hand, *they* might have gotten stuck with a little brother like Tyler.

No. Not with Mom and Dad in charge.

When we finally got home, Tyler had not dried off a bit. Despite all the pounds of mud and water that had dripped off him, he was still soaking wet. I brought him in the back door so he wouldn't drip mud on the living room carpet. I herded him upstairs. His tennis shoes still squished.

I figured my sisters would be furious over what had happened. Boy, did I get a surprise.

Hannah looked at him. Then she snickered. She giggled. She laughed. She howled with laughter. She couldn't quit laughing. She did manage to get out, "The duck pond!" amid the laughter.

Catherine laughed just as hard and long. Finally, when Hannah went off to ride herd on Bethany, Catherine said, "Wash him off in the tub, and I'll put his clothes in the dryer."

From the other room, Hannah yelled, "Run them through the rinse cycle first."

So bit by bit, step by step, we got Tyler back to looking half decent. He didn't cooperate in any of this, understand. I had to physically stick him in the tub and hold him down while Catherine washed him off. A lot of shrieking accompanied all this.

When it came time, at last, for him to get dressed again, he refused. "I'm not wearing those clothes. They have duck dirt on them."

"No, they don't," Catherine said. "We washed it off."

"They still have some!" he insisted.

Brute force won. I held his arms straight up while Hannah pulled his T-shirt down them. "Look at it this way," I told him, "If duck dirt is so bad, why did you want to catch the whole duck?"

He must have stopped to think about that, because he stopped struggling a moment. We took advantage of that moment to slip his shorts on him.

His mom was forty-two minutes late coming to get her dear children. As Tyler and Bethany fought over which one of them got to ride in the front seat, my sisters and I watched from the porch.

"He's gonna give his mom a real earful tonight, you know," I said. "She might fire you over this."

"No, she won't." Hannah looked just plain frazzled. "We're not that lucky."

"I wish I could have seen him fall in," Catherine said wistfully. "That would have been so great."

"Oh, it was, Catherine," I assured her with warm and heartfelt enthusiasm. "It was!"

9

I almost wished I knew what Tyler told his mom about his afternoon by the duck pond. Almost, but not really. Some things are better left unknown. However, either he didn't tell her much or she decided the cheap baby-sitting was worth half drowning her kid. Because the next morning, twenty minutes early, Tyler and Bethany were on our doorstep, whining as usual.

As they came trooping into the house, Tyler said, "Hi, Les."

Hannah and Catherine and I gaped at each other. It was the first polite greeting any of us had ever heard from him.

"Hi, pal. Neat dinosaur shirt. I like the picture on it. That's a Parasaurolophus, right?"

"Yeah. You like dinosaurs, too?"

"Yeah." I didn't tell him that my enthusiasm for dinosaurs had cooled off a lot, ever since I discovered airplanes. "Awesome monsters, no doubt about it."

I was referring to the Boeing 767, but I figured that wasn't something he'd understand. I didn't want to confuse a five-year-old.

"You know those toys we brought?" he shouted.

"Seven boxes of them."

"Come on up. Let me show you." He

47

grabbed me by the wrist and started up the stairs.

The Gang was going to meet in half an hour or so, but I had fifteen minutes before I had to leave, so I went up with him.

He sure had the plastic dinosaurs, all right. One of the seven boxes I had carried in was nothing but dinosaurs, except for a plastic volcano. They weren't the cheap ones, either. These were the big, solid ones, designed according to the latest information.

"So what's your favorite?" I asked.

"Tyrannosaurus rex."

It figured.

Something crashed in the other room. Bethany was being Bethany. Tyrannosaura regina, I suppose, would be the female version.

We talked dinosaurs awhile. I admired his action figures, and he explained minute details and facts. And you know what? Get him going on his favorite subject, and he was actually a halfway decent little kid.

"I gotta go now, Tyler. I'm meeting some friends in a couple minutes."

"I don't want you to go. Stay here and play dinosaurs with me."

"You know what an appointment is? It means you agreed to show up somewhere, so you show up. I agreed to show up, so I have to. But I'll come home for lunch, and we'll play then. I promise."

Me and my big mouth. Why did I say that?

He held onto my arm and tried to keep me

there. I peeled him off and left. He was shrieking as I went out the door. As I said, Tyler owned America and figured that any American should always do exactly what he wanted. Catherine held him to prevent him from coming after me. I strapped down my helmet, hopped aboard, and biked lickety-split to Sugar Creek Park.

All the same, I was the last one there. We chained up our bikes and filed into the woods, trying to look very respectful of this precious natural resource.

We saw nothing of a lady in hiking boots.

Tiny took over the project for two reasons: one, he was oldest, and two, he was a good organizer. "OK," he said, "we're looking for any sign at all of something bigger than a pond turtle. We're looking for tracks, some indication of a nest, gnawed bones, anything."

Lynn said, "I'm not sure I'm sharp enough to know what I'm seeing. I'll miss something."

"We can all say that, especially if Les is right and this really is some unknown animal. It might have signs we can't recognize. So we'll split up into two teams. Bits, you and I can go around to the far side of the creek. Mike, you and Lynn and Les work this side."

"Great idea!" I grinned. "'Cause even when you're right down next to the water, you can't see everything."

"That's right." Tiny nodded. "And we want to stay right down close to the water, too. Both teams will search along both sides of the creek bank. Let's stay across from each other. You guys watch our side, so you can see things we can't, and we'll watch your side."

And he and Bits took off to the little Swamp Loop bridge.

We waited until they worked back this way. When they came clambering down the bank on the other side, we started. We moved slowly, examining every nook and cranny, looking at all the mud. I found a few tracks, and Mike found lots of tracks, but we saw nothing that suggested a *big* animal.

Staying on the shore close to the water was tough. The vegetation was thickest there, right at the water. Dense brush, some of it poison ivy, entangled our legs, grabbing our knees and ankles as we tried to walk. We had to be careful not to step on wildflowers. We also had to be careful not to get so close that one foot would slip in the mud and we'd go in.

I thought again of little Tyler's slipping. How loudly would my sisters laugh if *I* came home soaking wet? I didn't want to think about it.

Mike picked up a fairly long stick. Whenever we came to a patch of reeds, he'd probe it with the stick. I saw Tiny doing the same on the other side. Bits was so reckless about where she walked, I was sure she'd be swimming any minute.

The going was very, very slow. Mostly, though, that was because we didn't want to miss anything.

We scared up a whole bunch of frogs. They

would plop into the water ahead of us, then surface right where the water met the land, with only their noses sticking out. We saw water striders and whirligig beetles and pounds of dragonflies. Even if we found no evidence of monsters at all, it was a great day.

But evidence of something was there. Mostly the water flowed straight along. But here and there along the sides of the creek, the bank would shrink back and form a sort of eddy—a wide spot. Sometimes the wide spot would be filled with reeds. I came to such a place.

"Hey!" I yelled across the creek. "There's green feathers floating back in this eddy!"

"From what?" Tiny asked.

I couldn't reach them, but I could get a good look. "From a green heron, it looks like. A shitepoke. Also there's a lot of long blades of grass floating."

"Fresh cut?"

I looked at Mike, and we reexamined the grass just out of reach. "Prob'ly not," Mike called to him. "It's pretty yellow."

We inspected that area especially carefully, but we didn't find anything else.

Now, a green heron is not a really big bird, but it's no puny little runt, either. To grab and kill a green heron requires a pretty big carnivorous monster. This led me to wonder how much the creek was hiding, and a tingle went up my spine.

Tiny reported seeing more grass blades floating on our side, but we couldn't see them.

We worked our way past the Swamp Loop bridge and on up the creek. We poked into every square inch, almost.

I was stooped over with my nose practically on the ground when a man's harsh voice yelled, "Hey! You kids!"

I stood up.

Two police officers were hurrying toward us, having a terrible time beating their way through the dense brush.

The first to reach us was panting a little. He pointed to Lynn, to Mike, to me. "You three! Lace your fingers behind your heads. You're under arrest."

10

So here we were being escorted away from the creek and back to the main trail by two police officers. Were we scared? What do you think?

Poor old Lynn was in tears. She wasn't crying out loud, but they were running down her cheeks. I glanced off toward the other side of the creek. Tiny and Bits had disappeared.

Why did they arrest us and not those two? I wasn't going to ask. Maybe these policemen didn't know that Tiny and Bits were over there. I sure wasn't going to give them any hints that there were more than three of us.

They stuffed us into the back of their police car. And as we drove away, I saw the old woman in hiking boots. She stood by the trailhead watching us leave, and she was smiling.

Lynn was slurping her nose because she didn't have a tissue. Mike looked grim and tight-lipped. And I imagine I looked totally scared, because I was.

This was a perfect time for prayer, but I didn't know exactly what to pray. One thing was sure. I didn't want to embarrass my parents, and I didn't want to embarrass Jesus. And it looked as if both things were about to happen. So that's mostly what I prayed about.

The fear and the praying didn't mean I wasn't thinking. What were we doing wrong? On the list of no-nos they posted in the park, getting off the trail was not one of them. We sure were not damaging anything or pestering the wildlife, except for an occasional frog. So why did they arrest us?

At the police station, they took us in a back door I had never seen before. The two officers sat us down on a bench by a desk. I assumed that the man behind the desk was a desk sergeant such as you read about in mystery books.

"Malicious mischief," one of the arresting officers said, and the two left.

"OK," said the desk sergeant. "Names."

We provided them.

By now I had about figured it out. That woman had seen us walking along the creek bank and assumed we were doing damage. She called the police. But we hadn't done anything, and no one had asked us if we did. No Miranda rights or anything like that. That meant that perhaps this wasn't a real arrest. They were trying to scare us, and they were doing a mighty fine job of it, too.

The desk sergeant didn't even look at us. "So which one of you is going to call your father?"

I reached for the phone. "Sir, I'm going to call my lawyer."

"Oh, you are." The way the man looked at me, I knew what he was thinking: *You smart-mouth.* Even though he didn't say it out loud. "What's his name?"

"William Walker, sir."

He held the receiver while I dialed. I punched in Dad's office number but not the extension.

The policeman put the phone to his ear. The look on his face changed. One moment he was sneering at me, and the next moment he looked surprised. I knew why. The receptionist had answered with the law firm's name. "Talbot, Cray, and Walker" sounded pretty high-falutin.

The policeman frowned as he asked for William Walker. He waited. "Mr. Walker, this is Officer Andrews. We're holding your son." Another pause. The frown deepened. "Sir, this is not a laughing matter." Pause. "I can't do that, Mr. Walker." Pause. The officer looked at me. "Outback."

I answered instantly, "You silly old galah."

Now there was a reason for all that nonsense. I learned later that Dad wanted to speak to me, and the officer said I wasn't allowed to. And when something really weird like that was going on, Dad and I had a password. He'd say "Outback," which is what Australians call their desert area, and the response was also a sort of Australian phrase.

And incidentally, a galah, pronounced guh-LAH, is a big, pink cockatoo, very common in Australia. It's also slang for a foolish person.

Anyway, that sort of told Dad that the call was for real. He must have said to the officer that he was coming, because the man said, "Thank you," and hung up.

"You kids sit right there until he gets here."

We did. You better believe we did. One of the woman officers brought Lynn some tissues for her nose. Lynn thanked her in that sweet, quiet voice of hers.

When Dad walked in, Lynn seemed almost happier than I was to see him. He really looked professional, too, in his white shirt and tie, carrying his briefcase and all.

He marched right over to the desk sergeant. "I want to talk to the arresting officer, please."

"That's not possible. They—"

"You can make it difficult, or we can get past this quickly. I'll wait." Dad sat down.

Grumpily, the officer looked up a number on a sheet and dialed it.

I was getting really antsy, but Dad was the soul of patience, so we all just sat there. Dad didn't speak to us.

The officers who had arrested us arrived.

Dad introduced himself. "I'm representing these three children. What are the charges?"

"Malicious mischief."

"And you saw them in the process of committing the mischief."

"No, sir, they were observed by a third party."

"And has this party filed charges or signed a statement?"

"No, sir, we—"

"Nothing on paper. How long did you personally observe them before arresting them?"

"A minute or two."

"And in that time did they do anything at all contrary to law?"

"They were off the trail."

Dad looked at me.

"The rules posted on the board don't say anything about that," I told him.

Dad nodded. "What manner of mischief, specifically?"

"I don't know, sir."

"So you arrested them on hearsay."

"Actually, sir," the officer said, "they are not technically under arrest. We detained them to—"

Mike interrupted. "You told us, 'You're under arrest.'"

"But they haven't been booked on an offense, is that right?" Dad looked from officer to officer.

"If you're a lawyer," the desk sergeant said, "you know the difference between arrest and detaining—"

Mike insisted, "But you said 'arrested'!"

The other officer spoke for the first time. "Basically, sir, we wanted to scare them so they'd stay out of the park."

"They're not going to stay out of the park," Dad said. I could read his voice. He was mad. I don't think the officers realized it. It wasn't noticeable unless you knew him really well. "If you have charges, declare them."

"They were damaging the park proper—"

"You don't know that." Dad softened his voice. "How do you know that the person accusing them doesn't simply have a grudge against one of them and is using this means to get even? How do you know the person actually observed improper behavior and did not leap to an assumption instead? For example, the person might be assuming all children are destructive. How do you know that the person can see well enough to correctly assess the children's behavior?"

I won't go into all the rest of it. Dad laid it on for another couple of minutes, using very high-tone words. He said something about enjoining them, and I had no idea what that meant. He let them know that we were really very protective of the park, which was true, and he let slip that we had even named ourselves after it—the Sugar Creek Gang. The end result was, the officers apologized—not to us, but to Dad.

We followed Dad out the door. Out the front door this time.

The first thing he asked was, "How come they didn't grab Tiny and Bits? Weren't they with you?"

"Yeah, we were." From beside the door, Tiny lurched to his feet. Bits fell in behind him, and they walked with us.

Bits said, "When we saw the cops, Tiny said, 'Duck,' and I didn't ask why. We were down in the weeds when the cop yelled, and they never saw us."

"They probably weren't looking across the creek anyway," I suggested.

Then Dad invited us for ice cream, and, somehow, we just couldn't bear to turn him down. We went with him to the world's greatest little ice cream stand a few blocks over.

The five of us took turns licking our ice cream before it could drip and telling him all about our search plan and how we were executing it.

He grinned. "Pretty smart, doing both sides at once."

"Yeah," Mike added. "And, Mr. Walker, we really were being careful. We were trying not to step on stuff that we could hurt, and we weren't bothering animals or things, not even bugs."

"Mr. Walker? Do you believe there's a monster in the creek?" Lynn asked.

"Yes and no," he replied. "I believe something very big scared the willies out of Bits. I don't believe it is an unknown monster."

Tiny smiled. "So you say we're dealing with a known monster."

"Something like that. An interesting possibility to pursue anyway."

"You worried me, though, Dad," I said. "When you said we were the Sugar Creek Gang, I was afraid they'd arrest us all over again."

He looked puzzled.

"I remember you said that gang activity is a misdemeanor in this town. And we're about as active a gang as you can find."

"Amen to that." And he didn't look especially thrilled about having to get such an active gang out of jail.

11

Dad was still mad that night at dinner as he told Mom and my sisters about our questionable adventures. "They might be kids, but that's no excuse for stepping on their basic rights!"

Then we discussed the old lady in the hiking shoes. When I said I was sure it had been she, Dad replied, "Well, *don't* be so sure. It's the easiest thing in the world to make a false assumption. You kids were detained on a false assumption. Don't fall into the same trap by making assumptions about somebody else. They might not be true." But then he added, "All the same, try to get her name next time."

The next morning I ate breakfast really fast and left the house before Catherine and Hannah could ask me to take Tyler again. Avoiding Tyler meant avoiding my own home. But where could I go? Then I got an idea.

I knew what I'd do: I'd go out to the animal rescue shelter and visit Tiny. Tiny had one of the world's great jobs. He was a volunteer at a shelter that took in injured wild animals, and he was on duty that day.

The shelter was way out of town. You rode and rode and rode to get there, particularly because Mom and Dad didn't want me on the main highway, so I had to go on back roads.

But it was even fun to get to. You biked in the gate and back a lane. There sat an old farm that used to raise chickens. In the long, narrow chicken sheds, they had set up some veterinary-medicine rooms and cages for sick animals. They used the inside cages in winter. The sheds were unheated, but, still, it was protection.

The yard too was full of cages, used mostly in summer. They were cheap, ratty things built of scrap lumber and chicken wire. But if you were an injured fox or rabbit, those cages did just fine.

As I wheeled into the farmyard, Tiny was just finishing up the feeding. He was hauling dishes and buckets around in a red coaster wagon. Usually, he greeted me warmly. This morning he seemed cool.

"Hi," I said brilliantly.

"Hi," he said cautiously.

I dumped my bike and followed him around while he finished up. "Not many customers anymore." I could remember a day when every cage was filled.

"Yeah, isn't it great?" Tiny parked his wagon. "Most of the young animals are old enough to take care of themselves now. And no baby birds now. They're all fledged. But I suppose we'll get more when the second nesting starts hatching."

I tagged along behind as he went inside. I'd helped many a time, so I knew where and how to put stuff away. I put the feed dishes in the dishwasher, added the soap, and turned it on.

Once breakfast was cleaned up, there was nothing more to do. "So," I said, "what's wrong?"

"Nothing."

"You could stand to be a little friendlier."

"I'm afraid you're mad at me."

"Item one, do I look mad? Item two, *why?*"

"For hiding when you got busted yesterday. I hid like a scared rabbit."

I thought about that a moment. "So let's say you didn't hide. Let's say you stood up and waved your arms and yelled, 'Hey, cops! Take me, too!' How exactly would that help?"

He shrugged.

I waited.

He said, "I'm ashamed anyway."

I really didn't know what to say. Tiny was always so logical and wise, and now here he was, being a kid. OK, he was a kid, mostly. Still, we Creekers depended on his being the most grown-up.

So I didn't say anything. I didn't know if it was right or wrong to let it drop, but I did anyway.

I waved a hand. "With not many animals to take care of, you have all this spare time on your hands. What do you do with it?"

"I'll show you." We left the main room, which served as both reception and veterinary exam room, and went into a room in the back.

Under a four-foot fluorescent light in the middle of the room sat a table. And on the table were half a dozen plastic ice-cube trays and a couple muffin tins. All were painted white. A thousand tiny bits and pieces had been sorted into the various ice-cube and muffin compartments. Sticks and basswood strips lay along one side of the table, and the middle was strewn with all kinds of tools. I had some of those tools in my own room for working on airplane models.

He picked up a boat model from a corner of the table. "This is my first try. It's the *Santa Maria,* Columbus's flagship. Plastic model. I bought the kit for fifty cents at a garage sale. It's not real good, but it came out OK."

Did he say, "OK"? It was beautiful!

"I like building ship models," he continued. "Now I'm building a model of the *Charles W. Morgan.* It's a whaling ship from about 1850. If it turns out OK, I'm going to try to carve a whale carcass and hang it on the side."

His *Morgan* model was a wooden one—wood hull, wood masts, and all. He had finished the deck furniture and had gotten as far as installing two of the three masts.

I looked more closely at the *Santa Maria.* Tiny had carefully painted a plastic figure of Columbus and glued it on the poop deck. I would not have known that the rearmost deck was the poop, but Tiny told me. He had learned the names of all the parts, even the rigging.

"That figure of Columbus looks awfully big," I said.

"Yeah. And look at these two sailors here." He pointed to one in the crow's nest, high on the mast, and another mopping the deck on the other side of the ship. "See? They're all the same size, and they go with the kit. So it was a really small boat."

"It's not even as big as a lot of yachts today. And they went clear across the ocean in that."

"And the *Pinta* and *Nina* are even smaller. The *Nina* was practically a rowboat."

Now I saw how the monster in the corner of my map could so easily bite a boat and snap it in two. It didn't even have to be a superbig monster.

"Columbus had guts and a half to set out in these things. I mean, what if all those monsters they used to draw around the edges of maps really were true? Maybe not exactly like the pictures, but—you know—kind of like that. Big. The point is, Columbus didn't know. He was taking a really big risk." I put the model down carefully.

Tiny flopped into the old wooden chair at the table. It creaked. He stared at the model for the longest time. "Maybe," he said, "we need to start taking some risks, too."

The idea didn't sound real appealing, since I was basically a scaredy-cat. Most of all, I wondered what kind of risks he was thinking of.

12

The next morning, I didn't get my breakfast eaten and escape quite soon enough. My sisters conned me into taking Tyler for another walk.

First we went to the neighborhood postal station to mail some stuff for Mom. We were inside the building less than five minutes. In those five minutes, Tyler managed to twirl every single knob that he could reach on the postal boxes. He got wedged behind a copy machine, and they had to move the machine to get him out. And he spilled a pamphlet rack.

Believe me, I just had to quit praying for patience!

We went over to Merrymount again. This time I went by a third route on back streets. The park experience lasted less than half an hour. He simply could not leave the poor ducks alone. I realize that park ducks have to get used to little kids, since so many small children visit the park. But this was ridiculous!

A landscaping crew came in. They dug a hole and planted a little tree near a stump where one had been cut down. I asked what kind it was.

The foreman said, "Red maple." He showed me how to tell red maples from other maple trees by the shape of the leaves. When I looked around, Tyler was pegging dirt clods at the ducks. I apologized to the foreman before I took off after him.

Finally, it was close to lunch. Well, close enough.

I wiggled a finger. "Come on, Tyler. Let's get started home."

"I don't want to go home."

"It's almost lunchtime."

"I don't want lunch."

"I don't want to miss it." That was a true story.

He ran off to the other side of the duck pond. I ran after him.

He headed for that sapling maple that the landscape crew had just planted. When I caught up to him, he yelled, "I'm not going!" and grabbed the tree. It swayed, and I was afraid he'd rip it right out of the ground.

"Yes, you are."

"No, I'm not." When I peeled him away from the tree, he took off at a run.

I may be skinny, but I can outrun a five-year-old. I caught him and clamped him under my arm, his kicking end sticking out forward and the head end out behind. His arms flailed and tried to hit me, but he couldn't. I am also not as strong as a lot of kids, and he was terribly heavy.

Still, I managed to carry him a block and a half. Have I mentioned that he shrieked a lot? He could have drowned out a fire-truck siren.

When I let him down, I kept a tight grip on his wrist. He tried lying down, so I dragged him along the sidewalk. He gave that up in a hurry.

I felt like praying, "Please, God, I'm perfectly happy with as much patience as I already have. I don't need any more, so please quit exercising my patience muscles so much!"

We finally got home, with him yanking and pulling and screaming the whole way. His sister, my sisters, and Mom were just sitting down to lunch when I got there. I plunked him in his chair and finally got to let go of his wrist. My hand felt stiff and achy.

Mom smiled. "We were going to go ahead and eat, but then we heard you coming."

"Yeah." Hannah glared with disgust at Tyler. "Fifteen minutes ago."

I knew she was exaggerating, since it's maybe a ten-minute walk to Merrymount. But she probably wasn't exaggerating by much.

Tyler poked around at his lunch and complained.

I didn't poke around. I finished as quickly as I could and stood up. "I did my bit. He's yours this afternoon."

"You can't do that!" Catherine shrieked.

"Oh, yes, I can." I took my plate to the sink. And I beat it upstairs to my room.

This monster business really had me intrigued now. Was there any other information that would give me a clue about what Bits saw in the creek? I tapped into some pretty good search engines on my computer and dug out references to monsters.

The Irish had some dillies. There were a lot of giants. When a magical horse whinnied, things went wrong. They had banshees, which were spirits that howled to announce a coming death. And of course there were the leprechauns.

It seemed that everybody in the world had sets of monsters all their own. North American Indians had Lewa, a monster that lived underwater and tipped canoes over. I checked that one out very carefully, but the Indians who believed in it didn't live this far south.

And I didn't believe in it, either. Whatever Bits saw was a real animal, not a mythical animal.

While I was at it, I also looked up Christopher Columbus. He sailed to the New World not just once but three times. The other two times, he had bigger ships. Apparently, the *Pinta*, the *Nina*, and the *Santa Maria* were pretty much the trash of Spain's fleet, because the king and queen didn't want to risk good ships on such a chancy venture.

Someone pounded on my door. Guess who.

"Let me come in!" Tyler yelled.

"I'll come out in a while." That was true. It would be suppertime in a couple hours.

"I want to come in! I won't break anything."

I didn't believe that any more than I believed in Lewa.

But finally I wanted a drink. I unlocked my

door and tried to slip out, but Tyler was too fast for me. The moment the door cracked open, he was inside my room like a shot.

He was in there for less than thirty seconds. And would you believe it? In that short time, he managed to grab the F-86 Thunderjet model I was building and break a wing off.

I was so mad I couldn't see straight. I hauled him out the door and didn't let him down until I had locked it behind me.

Then I got my drink and stomped down the stairs, still madder than a bear with a toothache.

I stuck my head in the den, where Mom was working at her computer. "I'm going out," I announced to her. "I'll be back by dinner."

"Where are you going?"

"Down to the Wildlife Service." And I added as I left, "I'm going to try to borrow a couple dozen darts and the tranquilizer gun they use on bears."

13

Did I really go out looking for a tranquilizer gun? Nah. Who would loan a tranquilizer gun to an eleven-year-old? Even if I could use it, which I couldn't. And wouldn't. But it sure was a great wish. Instead, I walked across the street to Bits's house. Maybe she'd be interested in a few video games.

Nope. She wasn't home. So I went down to Lynn's.

As I was about to knock at Lynn's door, here she came, wheeling into her yard on her bike. She had two plastic bags of groceries hanging from each handlebar. She might be a small girl, but she sure was strong.

She took them off her handlebars one bag at a time before she laid her bike down. I picked up the two that looked heaviest and helped her carry the groceries into her kitchen.

"I'm bored," I said, "and I can't go home."

She giggled. "Afraid you'll get stuck baby-sitting again?"

"Afraid I'll wring a certain little brat's neck." I described the latest outrage as we put cans away in the cupboard.

Lynn wagged her head. "What is his mom going to do when he starts kindergarten? The teacher is going to be on his case all day long. Or kick him out."

"Or when he's bigger than his mom and force won't work? I don't encourage him, and he's attached himself to me, anyway. Go figure."

"So you're bored. I really should practice my viola. But would you like to play a quick game of Monopoly first?"

There is no such thing as a quick game of Monopoly, but I said yes. Instantly, of course.

She cleaned my clock. I got Boardwalk but not Park Place, and she got all the yellow and red ones, which meant I paid double every time I went around the board. She didn't even have to buy a hotel in order to wipe me out.

I helped her put the game pieces and money away. "I guess it's the monster for me and the viola for you." And then, all of a sudden, I got a delicious thought. "Hey. Do orchestra musicians ever name their instruments?"

"Sometimes." She closed the lid.

"What's the name of yours?"

"I'm trying to think of something."

"I was looking up monsters on the Net and came across Irish ones. How about Banshee?"

"That's a monster?"

"When it screams, people die."

She stared at me a moment and burst out laughing. "That's perfect! My father is going to appreciate it, especially. Don't get me wrong— he encourages me. But if he's home, he always finds yard work to do when I start to practice."

I thanked her for the great game, and she

saw me to the door. As I left, I heard her tramping upstairs to tickle her Banshee in the ribs. I reluctantly headed home.

I made it to the top of the stairs and very nearly reached the safety of my room when Hannah came bursting out of hers. "Les!" she roared. "Go sit with Bethany a minute. I have to wash out Tyler's T-shirt." She gestured toward her room.

What could I do? I went.

In Hannah's room, Bethany had Barbie dolls and toys all over the floor. Her Barbie, I saw, had her own car, her own house with lamps that lit up, her own computer on her own desk, and her own Jet Ski. Whatever did an eleven-and-a-half-inch-tall doll need with a Jet Ski—especially since neither Bethany nor anyone else in her family played water sports?

Bethany sat on the floor with her legs bent in two and folded backwards. I don't know how she did that. She was manipulating a Ken doll, preparing to put him in the car.

I stood there, uncertain what to do. "So you have your Barbie out," I said lamely.

Bethany didn't even cast a glance my way as she cranked on Ken's legs. "Get me Ken's black leather jacket."

I sat down nearby. "Where is it?"

The way she looked at me, I could tell she valued empty gum wrappers more than she valued me. "In his closet, of course."

"Where's his closet?"

"Quit being nasty!"

"Look who's talking. Where's his closet?"

"Oh, you're so stupid! There!" and she waved a hand in the general direction of half the bedroom.

I thought about this for a few moments but very few. "Know what? If you want something, you can either ask nicely or get it yourself. Mom says normal courtesy is 'please' and 'thank you.' And as far as I'm concerned, unless you use normal courtesy, you're out of luck. Got it?"

I heard a shriek from the next room. Apparently normal courtesy was in very short supply up here.

"You can't tell me what to do! Get me his jacket!"

"You can't tell me what to do, either." I kept my voice cool and low, since hers was rising like a helium balloon.

And then, *powie!* She suddenly, right out of the blue, leaned over and slugged me! I didn't even see it coming. It hurt, too. It wasn't a playful punch the way Tiny and Mike and I sometimes bopped each other. Ours was friendly; we made sure it wasn't hard enough to truly hurt. Hers was out to get me.

Oh, man, that made me mad! It was all I could do to keep from slugging her right back. But I didn't. Partly, I was just so surprised that she did it.

Then if she didn't haul off to take a swing at me again! I didn't hit her, but I pushed her shoulder. She tipped back, and I stood up quickly. No use sitting there and letting her punch me twice.

Instantly furious, she screamed, flailing at me, but I stepped aside and headed for the door. I stood there in the doorway until Hannah came down the hall.

"The little creep is all yours!" I snarled, and I ducked into my room.

"Les! You can't leave yet!"

But my door was already slamming, and I was safe behind it. I locked it and stood in the middle of the room, all churned up inside.

What should I do? What should I have done? Could I have handled it better? Why did she do that? I really did not understand little kids.

I sat down on the window seat by my little dormer window. Now I may have mentioned sometime that this was my favorite place to pray in the evening. I liked it especially when the moon was coming up. I'd sit there and talk to God. Best of all, then I would just simply wait and listen, for usually God would talk to me.

It wasn't in words like two people chatting. It was more a quiet, unspoken knowing. I can't explain it. And it didn't always happen.

It didn't happen now. I sat. I waited. But this was still broad daylight, and it just didn't feel the same as evening. Eventually, I talked to Him. First I apologized for losing my cool. Then I asked His forgiveness for whatever I did wrong about the situation. I thanked Him for helping me to keep from blowing my top. I was pretty sure I would have lost it without His help.

I sat a while longer, but that special together feeling I sometimes had with Him wasn't here now.

So I got up and went over to my table. There I managed to get the broken wing put back on my fighter plane. Tyler had snapped off one of the wheels, too. I had a harder time getting that back on and looking right.

About five, I went downstairs to the dining room. Tonight I was supposed to set the table. I had the plates and the napkins out when Auntie Claire showed up for her little darlings, only twenty minutes late.

Mom answered the door and invited her sister in.

The instant Bethany saw her mother, the kid screamed. "Mommy! Mommy! Les hit me!"

I just about dropped a salad plate. What—?

Mom wheeled and stared at me through the living-room archway.

"I did not!" I protested.

Auntie Claire patted the little dear's head, soothing her with a soft, "There, there, dear."

I about threw up.

Mom apologized on my behalf. She said how sorry she was it had happened.

Then they left.

Mom marched right into the dining room. "Les, I'm ashamed of you. I realize there may have been some provocation, but you're four years older than she is. You should have—"

And for the first time in my entire life, I cut her off in midsentence. I was disappointed and mad. I was even madder than I had been at Bethany.

I yelled, "Thanks for sticking up for me, Mom!"

And then I ran upstairs to my room. I had already said too much.

14

At dinner that night, I didn't know what to say. I didn't feel like saying anything. I was still angry at the world and everyone in it.

After dinner, all Dad said was, "Les, come into my study."

I came. You didn't argue with Dad, ever.

He plopped into his favorite Naugahyde chair. "What's going on?"

That was something else. When he asked a question like that, you had better give him the straight, unvarnished truth, and you'd better not even slant it your way. If he heard differently, or got any hint at all that you were stretching the truth, you'd be in big trouble. And he could hear a false note quicker than anyone else I ever knew.

So, as best I could, I told him what had happened.

He listened without saying anything.

I shrugged. "I guess I'm still mad. And I'm also mad at those two kids because they're messing up our family."

"Are they messing it up, or are you letting them mess it up?"

I thought about that a minute. I knew he wanted me to say that I was letting them do it. But that's not what I felt.

"They are. The girls and I can put up with a little of that kind of stuff. In fact, we can put up with a lot of it. But sometimes it's just too much to swallow. We have a limit. Those kids pushed past the limit. Way past. Know what I mean?"

He nodded.

I sat quietly.

He asked, "What else is happening?"

Should I rat on Tyler breaking my plane model? I decided not to. We'd talked about Tyler and Bethany enough, as far as I was concerned. So I told him about Banshee, and he smiled. And I told him about Tiny feeling ashamed, and about the *Santa Maria*.

I finished up by saying that people sometimes liked to badmouth Columbus. "But he had real guts, Dad. And he got to the New World not once or even twice but three times. That's pretty good when you don't even have any good navigation instruments."

"I agree. How's your monster search coming?"

"I looked up monsters on the Net and didn't find anything useful. It could be anything."

Then Dad said, "The worst monsters are always human." And he wasn't smiling.

The next morning, I guess I still felt guilty for getting mad at Mom. I didn't understand myself. Anyway, for some reason, when Hannah begged me to take Tyler again, I didn't fight it. I took him. Besides, it was Friday. Beginning at dinner tonight, we'd have two whole days of rest from all this.

My assignment, as always, was to take him out and let him run off steam.

Predictably, Tyler said, "I want to go to the duck park."

"Not today." I took him in a different direction.

"Why not?"

"I feel too sorry for the ducks."

A familiar voice playfully called, "Beep beep!"

Here came Lynn on her bike. Her viola case was strapped on her back, sort of like a backpack.

She got off and walked along beside Tyler and me. "Hi, Tyler."

"Who are you?"

"Lynn."

"How do you know me?"

"You're famous. Having a good time, Les?"

"A peachy-keen time. Thanks for asking. Going to your Banshee lesson?"

She giggled again. "I told Daddy about that. He thinks it's great. Now we just call my instrument 'Banshee' around the house. I promised him I'd get past the banshee stage and learn to play well."

I thought, *And you really will, too.* Lynn could do anything she put her mind to.

"Well," I said, "I'd really like to help you with your lesson, but you can see that I'm busy."

"Pity." She sniggered.

"Hey. Even beginning viola lessons sounds

more appealing than sitting on this miserable little kid."

"I am not!" Tyler protested.

"Prove it!" I retorted. "Behave for a few minutes."

Lynn climbed back aboard her bike and, with a wave, tooled on up the street.

Tyler didn't feel like proving anything, I guess. His behavior didn't change a single inch.

About three blocks from our house was a shop called Small Stuff. It wasn't a real store. Rather, the living room of a regular house had been turned into a very small place that sold miniatures. It was crammed full of a little of everything—dollhouse stuff, model trains, planes, boats. I'd bought most of my airplanes there.

I knew better than to take Tyler inside. But I held onto his wrist, and we looked in the living-room picture window, which doubled as the store window. The owner noticed us and turned on the train that was set up in the window.

Tyler watched it for a good four minutes before he got bored. For him, that was something of a record. I waved thank you to the store owner and took Tyler on down the street.

"I want to go see the ducks!"

"No."

"I promise I won't chase them."

"No. Every time you promise not to do something, you forget your promise as soon as you have a chance to do it. Let the ducks rest in peace."

"I promise!"

"No."

Half an hour later, he was still bouncing off walls. Not that we were near any walls. I was walking him up and down streets yet. I was pooped. All my tires were flat. He was still full of steam.

And he was in a talking mood. There's nothing worse than a five-year-old with nothing to say and an urge to say it. He yelled nonstop about every topic under the sun. My ears were flat, too.

We sort of headed back. I figured we'd get home about lunchtime again.

Away down the street, I could see Lynn coming. She had her viola with her as usual. I figured she must be coming back from her lesson. It was about that time. But why was she walking her bike?

A white Toyota pulled to the curb beside her. It cruised alongside her at walking speed. I assumed that either the driver or a passenger was saying something to her.

It came to a parked car, swung out around it, and moved in close to the curb again.

I could barely make out that Lynn was shaking her head no.

Then the passenger-side car door opened. Lynn started walking faster.

I could see her face better now. She was scared!

She dumped her bike and began to race toward me.

"Come on, Tyler!" I yelled at the top of my lungs, "Lynn! Lynn!" as I broke into a run toward her.

For once I remembered to pray to God to help us. Too often I didn't think of praying in time.

I was close enough now to shout out the car's license number. I didn't even know why I did it until I realized that I wanted the driver to know he was identified.

The car door slammed. The Toyota's tires squealed as it whipped away from the curb and roared off past me and on down the street. I didn't get a good look at the driver.

I reached Lynn. I had never seen her so terrified, not even when she was arrested. She was gulping and sobbing so hard she couldn't breathe.

What could I do? I had no idea. So I just sort of hung onto her. That wasn't easy with Banshee strapped to her back.

She managed to say, "I was so scared!" She hiccupped between words.

"Sounds like you still are."

She might have been frightened, but she was a tough cookie. In a few moments she managed to pull herself back together. Slurping and snuffling, she wiped her wet face on her T-shirt tail.

Suddenly she stepped back and stared at me wide-eyed. "Wasn't Tyler with you? Where is he?"

"He's right h—"

Tyler was gone.

15

What a miserable bunch of people sat around in our living room. Dad had come home. His shoulders sagged. Mom was there. Lynn and her folks were there. Hannah and Catherine were there. The police had just left.

I heard brakes screech out at the curb. Dad leaped up and swung the front door open. His shoulders melted again. He stepped back.

Auntie Claire came storming in without even looking at him. I knew that Mom had called her. She was furious. Beyond furious. Instantly, she began screaming at Hannah, up one side and down the other, about losing her precious son. How could Hannah do such a thing? She trusted Hannah and now—

I interrupted her. "It was me, Auntie Claire. He was with *me*."

The chewing out didn't slow down a bit. She simply wheeled on me and continued her roaring tirade in midsentence.

And then Mr. Wing totally surprised me. He was a quiet man, very soft-spoken. Even when he raised his voice, which was almost never, you could barely hear him.

But now he jumped up and yelled, "Enough!" He even scared Lynn.

The room fell deadly quiet.

His voice dropped to its normal volume. "My name is Arthur Wing, madam. We have not been introduced, but I am going to tell you some things. This young man Les saved my daughter from terrible calamity. He may well have saved her life, in fact. He acted quickly and bravely. I understand that you are upset, but you will not pour out your frustration on him or on his sisters, either. They did not earn your anger."

Auntie Claire cried, "My son is missing!"

"And if Les had not stepped in as he did, in another few moments my *daughter* would have been missing. The driver was insisting that she get into his car."

Auntie Claire looked wild-eyed at Dad.

Dad nodded toward Bethany's chair. "Sit down, Claire." It wasn't an invitation.

Mom pulled Bethany out of the chair into her own lap. Auntie Claire sat down. Her face told everyone that she wanted to say more, but she didn't. She bit her lip.

Dad explained what happened. He told how Lynn got a flat tire on her way home from her lesson, so she was walking her bike. He described how the man pulled alongside her, said hello, asked where she was going, and in general made small talk. Then the man invited her to get in, promising he'd give her a ride to her door.

She said no. She wanted to stay with the bike.

He assured her that no one would steal a bike with a flat. Chain it to a pole and come on, he said.

She was getting suspicious. Now she told him to leave. That's when he opened the car door and insisted that she get in.

She was afraid he would reach for her, so she dumped the bike and ran. She said that he didn't really give up until he saw me coming.

Dad ended the story with, "Sergeant Ware and I were talking about this kind of thing just a couple days ago. The police had heard about someone in a white Toyota approaching a child. The man apparently said hello, chatted a moment, and suddenly drove on. Today was the first time he'd suggested that the child get in the car."

"The disabled bicycle was the perfect opening." Mr. Wing settled himself back in his chair. "He perhaps decided that this was the time."

Auntie Claire was still glaring at me. "That's all the more reason that you should have held onto Tyler!"

"But you don't know," I heard myself saying. "We all don't know." That needed explaining. "Dad says don't make assumptions, 'cause they can be wrong. He said this is a small town and that people in small towns are friendlier. Maybe the man really did mean to just give her a ride home. You know—a favor. We don't know what he intended."

"We were just talking about that recently. Glad you remembered." Dad smiled. "And Les is right. We don't know the man's motive. Lynn, you did exactly the right thing by not getting in the car. There are dangerous monsters loose in this world. But Les is also right that we can't judge someone without knowing. The two of you are showing a good balance: Don't judge a stranger, but don't trust him, either."

And I got a flashing thought. "Is that what Jesus meant when He said be wise as serpents and gentle as doves? Protect yourself from the bad guys out there, but don't assume everybody is automatically a bad guy."

"Maybe so. The problem now is—"

The doorbell rang. Dad got up and answered it.

There stood Tiny, Mike, and Bits. Dad invited them in.

"Dad called me," Bits said. "He said Tyler got lost, and we want to help find him." She looked around. "So why is everybody just sitting here?"

"Pull up a piece of floor," I offered.

"No. We want to go find Tyler."

So Dad and Mr. Wing explained the whole thing over again. Actually, I liked Bits's suggestion. Figure out something to do. Go. Get moving.

Mike asked the question we were all thinking. "You think Tyler might get in a car with a stranger?"

"Of course not!" Auntie Claire fumed. "He's much too smart, and I've told him not to."

Well, whoop-de-doo, my brain was saying. *Sure he'd get in a car with a stranger. He doesn't pay attention to anything anyone tells him, including his mom.* But I didn't say all that out loud. Auntie Claire was upset enough without me pointing out that her kids were undisciplined monsters.

I was getting pretty sick and tired of monsters.

16

Out in the garage, we had a squirt can of stuff that you sprayed into a flat tire through the air valve. Basically, it sealed up a puncture by spreading gunk all over the inside. So the five of us trooped out to the garage. I got the squirt can out, and we tried it. When we then pumped up Lynn's tire to its recommended forty pounds of air, the pressure held. She rode it half a block up the street and back. Still forty pounds.

While she was testing out her tire, Bits said, "Dad has a bolo out on the white Toyota."

"What does that mean in English?"

"All the cops have been told to look for it."

Tiny grunted. "Do you realize how many white Toyotas there are in this town?"

I said, "I sure wish Lynn and I could remember the whole license number. But she could remember only three of the numbers, and I could come up with only three numbers, and they were the same three."

Mike asked, "The cops are looking for Tyler, too, aren't they?"

Bits nodded. "They're covering that whole area where he got lost. Dad says they've asked the sheriff's search-and-rescue posse to come in. You know—guys on horses back all the alleys. But that takes a couple hours."

Wouldn't Tyler love to know he'd launched a horse brigade!

"You all been praying about this, right?" Tiny asked, almost accusingly.

"Yeah," I answered. "We did that first. And I sort of keep sending up a reminder now and then."

As Lynn came tooling up to us, Bits rubbed her hands. "OK. If you were Tyler, where would you go?"

I said, "To jail."

"Get serious."

And then it hit me. "Merrymount! He kept coaxing me to take him to Merrymount."

Mike grinned. "The ducks!"

Tiny frowned. "Out Oakdale? He'll get hit by a car."

"No," I replied. "I kept him on the back streets, trying to wear some energy off him. Never went the same way twice. He doesn't really know how to get there."

"Come inside." Lynn laid her bike down. "Back me up."

Back her up doing what? But I didn't ask. We were the Sugar Creek Gang. We backed each other up, period. We all trailed in through the kitchen to the living room.

Auntie Claire was ranting again.

Lynn ignored her. She marched right over to her dad. "Les's thingamajig worked. We got the tire fixed. Now we have some ideas about where to look for Tyler."

"I don't want you out on the streets right now," her mom told her.

"The five of us. Together we're safe, even if a bike breaks down. Please. We want to help."

"You haven't had lunch," my mom said.

I told her, "I'm not hungry."

So did Mike and Tiny. When Mike said that, you'd better believe his mind was on other things.

It was obvious that Mr. Wing wanted to say no. He hesitated the longest time. "I'm proud that you want to help, and that you're going about it sensibly. You children still think like children, and that may be exactly what we need here. To think like little Tyler." He pulled his cell phone off his belt and handed it to Lynn. "Don't lose it."

"Thank you, Daddy."

Without speaking, Dad gave me his. He also dipped into his wallet and gave me some money. He knew that, sooner or later, we'd get hungry enough to need it.

Mom was absolutely against the whole idea. You could tell it on her face and in the way she sat tense, as if wanting to jump up and scream. But all she said was, "Stay together."

"Yes, ma'am."

We hustled out before they could change their minds.

The minute we were through the back door and on the patio, Bits snatched the phone out of my hand. She punched in numbers. She listened as we gathered up our bikes. Once in a while, she'd punch another number. So she must have been caught in one of those answering machine menus. You know: "If you wish to talk to a representative, press one; if you think these answering tapes are nutty, press two . . ."

Then she picked her bike up off our lawn and spoke to the phone. "Hi, Daddy. The five of us think Tyler may have run away to Merrymount Park, but he doesn't know how to get there exactly. So we're going to look for him. We're together. Good-bye." She glared at the phone as she turned it off. "I hate voice mail!" She gave it back to me.

Tiny raised a hand. "Wait a minute. We're going to look for Tyler along the back streets between where you lost him and the park, right?"

"Right."

"How do you know that he didn't make a mistake and take off in the wrong direction? He's only five!"

"We don't know that. But I just had to get out of the house and do something to find him, and this seems like a good place to start." That sounded pretty weak when I said it out loud, but it was the truth.

"I agree with Les," Lynn added. "I couldn't just sit there talking about it much longer."

Mike shrugged, "It works for me."

So off we went.

Can you pray while you're riding a bike?

Sure you can. I did. And while I was asking the Lord for help, I knew that Lynn's folks and mine were all talking to Him, too. Maybe Auntie Claire was as well, if she could quit storming long enough.

We got pretty hungry, so we stopped at a fast-food place, because that's how you feed five people when you're poor. We pooled all our money, and we were still poor. On the other hand, we all got enough to eat, so therefore we were not poor. We were better off than a lot of people in the world.

"So Tyler really likes the ducks, huh?" Mike popped the last of his fries.

"Likes to chase them," I said. "He'd probably kill them if he could. That kid is the most destructive little tornado I've ever seen. And his sister is just as bad. They don't give a rip for anything or anybody."

Tiny stared off into space, looking thoughtful and chewing on his burger. Then he said, "You know, I think that's exactly what's wrong with that old woman who wants us out of Sugar Creek Park."

"She doesn't give a rip?"

"No. She just saw some kid like Tyler in the park—or maybe more than one like him. A kid or kids who don't give a rip and are destructive."

"I see what you mean," Lynn added, "and I agree. She sees a few senseless goof-offs and thinks that all kids are like that. Whether you're *doing* something destructive just then doesn't matter. I'm sure even Tyler looks ordinary once in a while, between the bad behavior."

Mike nodded. "So she sees us being ordinary and thinks we're gonna go kill another duck in just a minute."

Schraaaanck! Bits sucked the last of the drink out from under the straw in her cup. She frowned and shook the cup, maybe hoping more drink would fall through the ice to the bottom. "I'm on her side. I don't trust anybody."

"You're probably right, these days." I sighed. "Still, I wish I could tell when the right thing to do is to assume the worst about a person, and when you're just jumping to conclusions."

It would sure make life a whole lot simpler.

17

Whoever planned the streets around Merrymount Park used a plate of spaghetti for a model. Oakdale, which was straight except for two lazy curves, was the only sensible street in the area. Of course, it was a main route. All the little side streets sort of wandered in S shapes and came out at odd places. Many of them ended up as cul-de-sacs—that is, the street just quit. *Poof.* Gone.

Even if Tyler had a good sense of direction for a five-year-old, he could have gotten mixed up anywhere in that tangle. You'll recall I ended up on dead ends a couple times myself when I was taking him there.

As we got started again after lunch, Bits said, "Don't forget to keep an eye out for a white Toyota sedan."

Then we sort of split up into two groups. Lynn and I had phones. So Mike, the best tracker, went with me, and Tiny went with the girls. In other words, a phone in each group. For instance, they would go west on one little street, and Mike and I would go west a short block over. We stayed right across from each other and were usually able to see each other. That way we could check out twice as many little side streets in the same amount of time.

So far, we were covering a lot of ground, but we weren't getting anywhere.

My phone rang. I hollered to Mike and stopped to answer it. I couldn't talk on it and ride my bike at the same time. "Hello."

"Bits's dad here. Is your dad around?"

"Hi, Sergeant Ware. You can reach him at our home phone, I think. We're out looking for Tyler."

"Where?"

I asked Mike, "What street is this?"

"Hang on!" He pedaled to the corner, read the street signs and called back, "Poplar near Chestnut!"

"Poplar near Chestnut. I see Bits and Lynn and Tiny. They're coming this way on Chestnut. Mike just told Bits you're on the line. Here she comes. She's waving. I think she wants to talk to you."

She skidded to a halt beside me, and I handed her the phone.

"Hi, Daddy!" Pause. "Yes, we are." Another pause. "We'll call you right away. No, Daddy, we won't try to stop him by ourselves." She rolled her eyes skyward. "I promise. We won't play cops. Listen, Daddy? Can you send some cars over here?"

Why did she ask that? I wondered. Sergeant Ware must have asked the same question.

She answered both of us. "Because we talked to an old lady sitting on her porch. She said a little boy came by, all out of breath, about an hour and a half ago. He wasn't from her neighborhood. But by the time she got up, he was gone. That's a good lead, don't you think?" Pause. "North. OK, Daddy." Pause. "I love you, too." She turned the phone off.

"So somebody saw Tyler!" I felt good suddenly.

"Maybe. She thought the kid she saw was older than five, though."

"Tyler acts older. Hour and a half would be about the right time, too."

Tiny said, "I have an idea. In fact, it's more like a strong feeling. Tyler might have a better sense of direction than we gave him credit for. Maybe we should just go on over to Merrymount and see if he's there."

That sounded really good to me. "Sure. If he's not, we can start working our way back this way."

Lynn looked sad. "Almost two hours. That poor little boy must be so scared by now."

She didn't know Tyler.

So we hit the road again. Lynn's bike tire was holding up just fine.

A police car came cruising by. We all waved. The woman officer in the passenger seat waved back, grinning.

"That's Linda!" Bits said. "I think her partner's name is LeRoy, but I'm not sure."

I wondered what it would be like to know almost all the officers on the police force. Or most of the lawyers in town, like my dad. Or lots of professors, like Mr. Wing. Or . . .

I didn't even know any school kids yet

except the Creekers and a few kids in church, because my family had just moved into the area and I hadn't gone to this school yet.

That's probably also why I didn't know where all these crazy little side streets went. What a jumble.

A horn tooted behind us. I looked back. Mr. Ware was driving a black-and-white, and my dad sat in the passenger seat beside him. Excuse me—I guess when Bits's dad is in uniform and driving a police car, you ought to call him Officer Ware or Sergeant Ware, not Mister.

We all waved enthusiastically. Waving back, they drove on past us and turned right at the corner, so we continued straight ahead.

And suddenly, there lay Merrymount Park right in front of us! We were entering not by the usual way that I was used to but through a small gate at the north side.

Tiny assumed command. "Keep in sight of each other, but let's fan out some. The duck pond is down that way."

Good idea. We separated, keeping across from each other, but there were maybe fifty or seventy-five feet between us. If a bush hid an area from one of us, someone else might be able to see around it.

We bumped our way along the rough grass.

"Look!" From over by Tiny, Lynn pointed wildly, not toward the duck pond but beyond it to a park bench way down in the far corner. The bench was partly screened by bushes, and at first I couldn't see from my angle. Lynn had spotted him, though.

Tyler sat on the bench, swinging his feet and talking to a park visitor.

We were still pretty far away. The man got up, and Tyler slid down off his seat. The two of them started walking our way across the grass.

But they weren't walking toward us. They were walking toward the gravel parking lot.

And parked there was a white Toyota sedan.

18

Tyler!" I yelled. "Hey, Tyler!"

The man seemed not to hear me, but Tyler did. He looked all around. We were still pretty far away, and it took him a moment to see us. Then he waved his arms like a conductor trying to stop a symphony orchestra.

Now the man too saw all of us coming toward him. We must have been a weird sight—five kids on bikes ripping down the grassy lawn, abreast but widely separated, like a howling horde of barbarians. He stopped cold and stared.

Tyler seemed to be talking. He was still gesturing enthusiastically.

I dropped down a gear and sped up the pedaling, trying to make better time across the grass.

Bits and I were both bearing straight down on the pond. If we didn't turn, we'd go into the water. We moved farther apart; she went around one side of it, and I went around the other.

I couldn't help but notice that the ducks were all huddled protectively in the very middle of the water. They swam in tight, cautious little circles as far from shore as they could possibly get. It was a sure sign that Tyler was here.

The man looked bigger standing up than

he had in the car. But then, I had not really gotten a good look at him before. We were getting close enough to see their faces now and hear loud words, many of which Tyler was spewing.

You would think that a new friend of Tyler's would see us and say something like, "So those are your little friends." Or maybe he'd sneer at us. Maybe he'd ignore us. At least you would think that he wouldn't look alarmed. The man acted as if he feared us.

Lynn shouted, "That's the man! I'm sure!"

He broke away from Tyler then and shifted into a lumbering run toward the parking lot.

Tyler took off after him. But as little kids so often do, he tripped and sprawled forward. He landed right on his face. And I mean on his face. His arms and belly didn't catch him.

Bits and I both made a beeline for Tyler. So did Lynn. I noticed Tiny and Mike veer aside, though, and take after the running man.

Bits screamed, "Don't, Tiny! Mike! Come back! We're not allowed!"

The two of them broke off the chase and pedaled back toward us. What in the world would they have done if they had overtaken the fellow?

The man climbed into his white Toyota. In a second, the motor roared, and he backed out of his slot.

I tossed my bike when I got to Tyler. It's what you'd call a running dismount. About half the times I tried that, when my feet hit the ground they would fail to catch me right. So I had a 50 percent chance of falling flat on *my* face. Believe me, one of my messed-up dismounts was quite a sight to see.

This time, though, the other 50 percent won out. I got it right and hit the ground running.

Tyler was screaming. Was it pain, or rage, or frustration, or just because he felt like it? I didn't know. And I didn't know what to do. I did not do well with screaming kids. Do you hold him? Help him up? What?

All the same, I had never felt happier. I was just plain joyful! Tyler had gotten lost on my watch, and now here he was, found again. He was dead and now alive, as the story about the prodigal son says. I wondered if this was just a very small, teensy-tiny taste of what the prodigal son's father felt like. If so, the man must have been beside himself with joy. What was gained was so much greater in that case.

Still protesting loudly, Tyler climbed up on his feet without my help. What a mess his face was! He even had grass stains on one cheek!

Lynn hopped off her bike the normal way and simply wrapped her arms close around him. Mike and Bits and Tiny gathered around. They acted as lost as I felt.

"Look!" Beside me, Mike was pointing out toward the parking lot. Bits and I twisted to watch.

Halfway across the lot, the white car had stopped because it couldn't go anywhere. One police car, its lights dancing, blocked the front.

So the fellow couldn't go forward. Another police car penned him in at his back bumper. He couldn't go backward, either. And they were so close to him, he couldn't whip out around them.

I recognized Linda and LeRoy as they got out and approached the driver of the Toyota. From the car blocking the Toyota's front, Dad and Sergeant Ware got out. Bits's father nodded; he seemed to be running the show. Dad left the action there and came toward us. I had never known he could run that fast.

Dad threaded his way among bikes and kids. "You kids did well," he said. "Very well!"

Tyler wasn't exactly hugging Bits. It was more that he was letting her hold him a moment. Then he tried to wrench away, still yelling. "I want to go with him!"

Dad and I looked at each other.

Bits asked, "Why?"

"He has a puppy!" More wailing. "He said he'd give it to me!"

I grabbed Tyler by the shoulders. "There isn't any puppy!"

"Yes, there is! I want—"

"There is not! He was lying, Tyler! No puppy, or kitten, or anything! It's what bad people tell little kids, and it's never true!"

I wanted more than anything else to shake some sense into him, but you never, never, ever —absolutely never—shake a child for any reason.

I think maybe he half believed me. He still wailed, but he didn't try to pull away.

"Time to go home, Tyler," Dad said quietly. "Your mom's waiting." He picked the boy up.

Shrieking, Tyler arched his back and tried to kick. I couldn't imagine fighting Dad like that.

Then Tyler managed to slam Dad in the face with his hard little head. Dad almost dropped him. He clamped down hard and just held him.

I used Dad's phone to call Mom, delivering the good news. Then I told Dad, "She and Auntie Claire are on their way to get you and Tyler." It was hard to hear, the way Tyler was howling.

Dad started toward the gate. We walked our bikes beside him. Now, if we could all just keep from going deaf from the noise, we'd do fine.

19

Tyler was crying.

Bethany was crying.

Auntie Claire was crying.

Even Mom was close to crying.

Dad was close to yelling at them. He wasn't yelling at Mom, but since Auntie Claire was her sister, Mom was sitting in on the session in our living room.

Catherine and Hannah and I sat there, too. The girls looked just plain relieved that someone might finally be getting through to Auntie Claire that things could not go on as they were.

I couldn't remember a time when Dad ever talked the way he was doing now. It was as if a whole lot of stuff uncorked at once.

He was explaining to Auntie Claire the sheer need of discipline.

The worst monsters were always humans, he said. Talk about a monster. When the police, Sergeant Ware among them, ran a check on the man in the white Toyota, they found he had a long criminal record. In fact, he was out of prison on parole. Bits's dad called my dad and told him.

If we Sugar Creekers hadn't found Tyler when we did, the man would have taken him away. He talked about puppies a lot to lure little kids, then would kidnap them.

But if Tyler had come with me as I told him to when I ran after Lynn, he would not have fallen into danger. That, Dad said, was an important reason for discipline. Little kids just don't understand all the dangers there are out in the world. They need to be protected until they get old enough to protect themselves.

He used Lynn as an example. Her parents taught her never to get into a car unless they said she could. She obeyed them, and, as her dad said, she escaped disaster. Tyler and Bethany had to learn how to obey that way.

He used the Creekers and my sisters as examples, too. We didn't dump a job we hated —taking care of two out-of-control little kids— because we promised we would do it, so we did. When it came to finding Tyler, we stuck with it until we found him. And doing all that required that we discipline ourselves into doing it.

In other words, Dad said, to grow up as safely as possible and to grow up being able to handle what life dishes out, you have to have discipline.

He had never explained it to me like that before. I understood what he was saying, though.

He ended his long speech with, "Claire, we aren't criticizing or bad-mouthing you . . ."

It sure sounded like it to me.

He continued, "We're showing you a problem that is going to bring big trouble on you if you don't turn it around. It very nearly did today. We want to help you solve that problem."

Mom asked, "Will you let us help?"

Then she and Dad said it again a couple of different ways. They didn't want to meddle, but they did want to help.

Auntie Claire was still all broken up. "I see what nearly happened. I understand. But I spent my whole childhood being punished. I don't want that to happen to my children."

"Discipline isn't punishment," Dad replied. "Jesus' followers were called disciples for a reason. They were disciplined. They were not punished. They were trained. The Bible wisely says, 'Train up a child in the way he should go' . . ."

Then he and Mom discussed with Auntie Claire how to bring her kids under control.

I thought it was probably a lost cause. But maybe not. When Tyler was talking about dinosaurs, he was a sharp little kid. There didn't seem to be any reason he couldn't learn discipline. He just didn't feel like it.

I excused myself and left Auntie Claire and my folks to tame the monsters. I went upstairs to my room.

The old map still lay open on my desk.

Monsters.

And something very big in Sugar Creek.

I was hungry. Really hungry. When was Mom going to make dinner?

I worked on the fighter awhile. I got to the place where I could start applying decals—that is, if Tyler didn't manage to get into my room again and set me back by breaking it.

Boy, was I hungry!

I thought about reading, but you can't read well on an empty stomach. So I sat in my little window seat and watched the sun get lower and lower.

It made interesting light patterns on the trees out there, some gold and some bright green. The window faced east southeast (I got the heading from an orienteering compass when we first moved in). So sunrises and moonrises put the light right in my window. Now, with sunset coming, the sun was behind me.

I could talk to God, I thought. He's always ready to listen. And there was one thing I made certain I did. That was to thank Him. I thanked Him for helping us find Tyler. I also thanked Him for Tiny. When Tiny got that sudden feeling that we ought to go directly to Merrymount Park, we all acted on it immediately. Tiny's listening to that quiet feeling and then obeying it saved Tyler. That was a part of discipline Dad hadn't mentioned, but it was an important one, I thought. When God says to do something, do it!

I thanked Him for things like cell phones, too, which helped us get Bits's dad there.

What were the other Sugar Creekers doing? I thought I might pull down my e-mail and see if anyone was online to talk to. But I didn't feel like it.

Then Mom's voice floated up from downstairs, saying those wonderful words, "Les? Dinnertime."

I got halfway down the stairs before I remembered I forgot to wash up. I ran back up, did it really, really fast, and ran downstairs again.

I headed for the dining room. "I'll have that old table set in a jiffy, Mom. Are Auntie Claire and the kids staying for dinner?"

She laughed. "We're all going out. It's been a harrowing day, and nobody feels like cooking."

That suited me!

So we all piled into Auntie Claire's van, and she drove us to a good cafeteria nearby.

Years before, I had learned the phrase "ulterior motives." That means that when someone did something, the reason he gave for doing it wasn't the real reason. At least, it wasn't the only reason. There was a hidden reason besides.

I decided as we got out of the van at the cafeteria that Dad and Mom maybe had an ulterior motive in taking Auntie Claire and us out to dinner. They wanted to show her what firm, loving discipline looked like.

I was more interested in eating than in keeping Tyler and Bethany walking in a straight line.

Things went fine for a while. We didn't talk about Tyler's run to Merrymount. That had been talked about enough, with each other and with the police.

Then Tyler decided he wanted Bethany's roll. So he grabbed it. When Mom made him give it back, he shrieked with that high-pitched screech of his.

Instantly, Dad stood up, grabbed him, and hauled him out of the dining area toward the lobby. Auntie Claire looked stricken, but she didn't say anything.

"Les," Mom said, "take your father's dinner out to him, please."

"Tyler's too?"

"No."

I scooped up Dad's plate and flatware and followed them out. What was going on? I had no idea.

Tyler was still screeching, but he was doing it on a bench in the lobby. Dad was using a leg to pin him down to sitting. I set Dad's plate beside him—on the opposite side from Tyler. While Tyler threw his conniption, Dad started to quietly finish his dinner. He talked to Tyler in a smooth, soothing voice, while the kid cried and screamed and begged.

I went back inside to finish my own dinner. The noise in the lobby calmed down eventually. As I was scooping up the last of my chocolate pudding, Dad and Tyler came walking back in. Tyler sat at his place and started eating again. Dad sat at his and nursed a cup of tea. No one said anything about behavior.

Bethany looked scared. I knew why even without asking her. She had no idea what had gone on out in the lobby. All she knew was that

Tyler seemed properly subdued. And I knew that she knew that if *she* stepped out of line, she would be next.

What a delight to see!

20

The doorbell rang at 8:00 A.M. on Monday morning. It wasn't Auntie Claire. She had dropped the kids by twenty minutes earlier.

"Look what we found!" There stood Tiny and Mike on our front porch.

I invited them in.

"I was humming around the Net, and I decided to check out monsters," Tiny said as they came in. "Found this." He handed me a Xeroxed magazine article. "So when my folks and I went to the library yesterday, I looked it up in *Canoe and Kayak*."

"Why *Canoe and Kayak*? Come on upstairs." I led the way.

"It puts a whole different spin on monsters," Mike crowed as he jogged up the steps.

The title was "Below There Be Monsters," and under that was "A Savvy Kayaker's Guide to the Hideous Beasts Lurking Beneath."

It even talked about my personal favorites, serpents that wrapped around ships. It talked about the pretend monsters of myth and then the modern-day true-life ones. Mom brought apples up to us as a snack, even though I'd only finished breakfast half an hour before. It was nice of her, and we thanked her.

We sprawled all over the floor. None of us really used furniture much.

While Mike and Tiny went through my *Natural History* and *National Wildlife* magazines, I read the article. It talked about an octopus twenty feet from tip to tip. Orcas that really are killer whales. Leviathan and cachalot, which are crocodiles, and sperm whales. It was great.

I gave it back to Tiny. "Most of them are salt-water things, though—animals that sea kayakers might come across. Not much about creek monsters."

Then I raised a finger. "Hey, listen."

"I don't hear anything." Mike frowned.

"Exactly." Maybe this discipline business might work after all. As Tiny and Mike and I lounged around in my room that morning, we didn't hear any shrieks or crashes down the hall for over an hour. It was some kind of record.

Tiny was flaked out on the floor, eating the last of his second apple. "I have an idea about the monster in the creek."

I grinned. "I remember when you didn't believe Bits."

"I changed my mind. It's more fun to believe there's a monster than that there isn't a monster."

"What's your idea?" Mike asked.

"Bits saw it early in the morning. Maybe the reason nobody else has seen it before now is that it's nocturnal—out only at night. So we go down to Sugar Creek after dark . . ."

"Nope." Mike sat up and tossed his core at the wastebasket. Scored two points. "Mama don't let me out after dark."

"I don't think my mom and dad would let me do that, either," I said. "And it's for sure that Bits and Lynn wouldn't be allowed. Next idea."

Tiny sniffed. "And just how do you intend to find it if it is nocturnal?"

"I don't know. But here's another knot in your shoelace," I said. "The park is closed at night."

Someone knocked on my door.

"Is that Tyler?" Mike asked.

"Can't be. The door is still standing." So I went to see.

Bethany stood there. "Can I come in? Please?"

Here were three boys all bigger than she was. If she headed for something breakable, surely one or more of us could stop her. How much damage could she do? So I said yes and stepped aside.

She marched in and plunked herself down among us. Her voice dropped to a low, throaty whisper. "I heard what you said. You're going to the park after dark."

"No, we're not."

"You are too. I heard you. I want to go along."

"We're not going," I said for the third time.

She didn't seem to hear as well as she thought she did. Or maybe it was just that she didn't listen as well as I expected her to. "I want to go, too."

"We're not going."

That squeaky little voice rose. "You're just saying that so that you don't have to take me! I want to go. It'll be fun! I'll keep up."

"We're not going."

"I'll spend the night here, and you don't even have to come to the motel for me."

"We're not going."

"You know," Tiny said, "you act pretty grown-up, if you're only seven and you don't mind staying away from home at night."

"I am grown-up! And besides, we're not home. We live in a motel."

Mike cooed, very patiently, "I'm not sure, but Les just might have mentioned that we're not going. I'm bigger than you, and *I'm* not allowed out at night, so neither are you. Our parents said."

She said, "You can sneak out. It's easy."

"Sure, it's easy," Tiny agreed. "And our bikes won't make any noise when we ride away. And if we're quiet enough, we might even get to see a monster in the creek. Except we're not gonna."

She started to protest.

I cut her off. "Hey, Squirt. Remember what Dad said last night? Obey your parents, because they know what's best for you. So we're obeying our parents."

"But they won't know!"

"That's not what obedience is all about. It's

about doing what they say, whether they know you're obeying or not."

"And," Tiny added, "you're supposed to obey God the same way—doing it just because you're supposed to. Except that He always knows everything, down to your deepest thoughts."

"You're just saying that so you don't have to take me."

I was going to say we weren't going, but why bother?

She pouted. "If you don't take me, I'm gonna tell."

Mike and Tiny and I looked at each other.

"Tell what?" Mike asked.

"I'm gonna tell your mommy that you're sneaking out. I'll say I heard you talk about sneaking out. I'm gonna tell what you're going to do."

"We're not going to do it." There, I said it again.

"I'll tell! I really will."

"Tell you what," I said. "We'll let you know if we decide to go." I stood up and ushered her to the door. "Believe me." I gave her a gentle push and closed the door behind her.

And locked it.

"Les! Let me in!" She pounded on the door.

I went back to the piece of floor I'd been sitting on. I picked up Tiny's article to look at the pictures again. Great pictures of octopuses. Octopi? Whatever more than one of them is called.

"That's amazing." Tiny flopped back to lying down. "Is she always like that?"

"Nah. Sometimes she's worse."

21

I thought about a lot of things that Monday. Part of what I thought about was how to visit Sugar Creek at night. Another part was Bethany's threat to squeal on us.

Tiny said to just forget about it, because we weren't really going to do it anyway.

But he didn't know—because I hadn't told him—that when Bethany accused me of hitting her, Mom believed her. That still bothered me. It bothered me a lot. What bothered me most was that it just might happen again.

"The best defense is a good offense," someone once said. In other words, to protect yourself, attack.

So after Auntie Claire carried off Bethany and Tyler for the day, and we sat down to dinner, I told Mom and Dad about Bethany's threat.

"Why, that little blackmailer!" was all Mom said.

I carefully explained that we were trying to figure out some way to explore Sugar Creek after dark. I hoped Dad would offer to help somehow. But he didn't. In fact, he had some kind of big case coming up and was distracted a little. After dinner he closed the door to his study and put out his needlepoint Do Not Disturb sign.

Obviously, if we Creekers were going to find a nocturnal monster, we would have to do it ourselves. But how?

That night I didn't go right to bed. After I turned out my light, I opened my little dormer window and just sat there awhile, looking at the night.

It had been raining off and on through the day. Now lightning and thunderheads were messing around in the sky. All you could see, though, were occasional zaps of whiteness among the clouds. You couldn't see actual lightning bolts.

Apart from the occasional barking dog, I heard a strange chirring sound far away. Then I heard it calling closer. It sounded like a bird with a frog in its throat. What could it be? Aha! Screech owl.

I thanked God for that screech owl. It was neat to know an owl lived nearby. And I thanked Him for good friends. Tiny and Mike came to mind right off. I thanked Him for my family, which was a really good, caring family even if Dad didn't volunteer to swat mosquitoes along Sugar Creek.

I thanked Him again for keeping Tyler from harm. I sat in the dark then and just sort of . . . well . . . sat there. We didn't carry on an unspoken conversation, God and I, as we did some nights. But we sort of hung out together without communicating. It was exactly the way Mike and Tiny and I often did. We could enjoy each other's company without saying anything.

When I found myself dozing off, I hit the sack.

The next morning, Auntie Claire dropped the kids off a little before 7:30. Hannah hadn't eaten yet, and Catherine was still half asleep. They were not pleased. But apparently Tyler and Bethany hadn't eaten either. Feeding them breakfast killed a whole hour, which made my sisters very happy. That made it one hour sooner, you see, until the little darlings' mommy returned.

I pointed out to Hannah that she had based her baby-sitting offer on an eight-hour day. She was sitting about nine hours a day. That reduced her profits right there. Add to that the cost of repairing and replacing broken items, and she was losing money on the deal.

Hannah grumbled sadly, "Don't remind me."

Then Bethany started pestering me. She wanted to go to the park. Nothing else would do except go to the park. She wore on me for three hours until I finally gave in. We would go to the park.

Sugar Creek Park. I didn't feel like going to Merrymount. So I called up Lynn. Did she still have any bike helmets she'd outgrown? She did. Bethany and I went up to her house. She dug the largest of her outgrown helmets out of the rafters in their garage while Bethany whined and made a pain of herself.

We put the helmet on Bethany. It didn't fit.

"Then she can use my regular one," Lynn

said and loaned it to us. We tried that one on the little doll.

Bethany complained that she wanted to go.

"So how's Banshee?" I asked. I adjusted her chin strap.

Lynn giggled. "Banshee is fine, thank you. My father is frazzled, but Mama says we'll all survive. I've mastered five scales. I mean, I've nailed them. And I sort of know four others."

I assumed that was good.

Then Bethany kicked at me and said again that she wanted to go.

Lynn told her flat out, face-to-face, "You are such a spoiled child, you're no fun to be with."

Was it out of meanness that we lingered awhile talking? I hope not. But that's what we did. While Bethany grew more and more obnoxious, we talked about Tiny's idea that the monster might be nocturnal.

Then, finally, I sat Bethany on my crossbar, and we biked to Sugar Creek Park. We pulled into the picnic area, and I chained my bike to the rack. We left our helmets there, hanging from the chain. I didn't want Bethany throwing one of them into the creek.

Could she really do that?

Can a professional wrestler do sit-ups?

I had mixed feelings about the old lady in hiking boots. Mostly, I hoped desperately that she wasn't there. I didn't want to deal with that again. But in a way I wished we would meet her. Then Bethany could see—and feel—what it was like to get chewed out royally. The woman did a far better job of it than I or even Dad could.

We walked into the dark shadows of the woods. Despite that the sky was still overcast, the woods felt pleasant. They would have been silent except for the birds, if Bethany hadn't been there. She whined and asked questions every moment, nonstop. Sometimes, for want of anything better to say, she just repeated the same thing over and over: "I want to see something."

We walked along the creek trail, but she didn't think much of frogs that jumped into the water before she could see them. And the crawdad in its chimney ducked down too fast.

I angled off onto the Swamp Loop. There I led her out to the Creekers' special place and showed her the turtles on the log. A great blue heron took off from just upstream of us, pumping its huge, gray wings. The kingfisher flew past us with silver minnows in its beak.

She wasn't impressed. "I want to see the ducks."

"There aren't any ducks in this park."

"Why not?"

"A monster ate them."

How close to true was that? Pretty close, maybe.

"I wanna see ducks!" she yelled. But then she picked up a stick. Little kids can't resist sticks. She got interested in poking it in places along the shore.

Baby-sitting eased up instantly. All I had to

do was keep a constant eye on her so she didn't fall in. I could just see me coming home with yet another soaking-wet kid. She got her shoes all muddy, but I figured that was a small price to pay.

On the bank we found a dead fish—a sucker about ten inches long. It was probably a hogsucker. I showed Bethany its big fat lips. I showed her how its mouth would extend out when it ate.

I watched tree shadows darken the creek, making its muddy water look muddier. The kingfisher called from somewhere, but I didn't see it. Up in the trees, the cicadas began their nonstop chirring. So many things!

By now it was close enough to four-thirty that we could start home. "Time to go," I said.

"I don't want to."

Somehow I was expecting that. "Well, we have to anyway."

"I don't want to. Uncle Bill hates me."

Now, I sure wasn't expecting that. "My dad loves you and wants you to stay safe."

"No, he doesn't." She stood up very tall to look me eye to eye, as much as she could. "He hates me! I know he does. My daddy hates me, too. He told me so!"

And I didn't know what to say to *that*. "Time to go."

I threw the dead sucker way out into the murky, gray-tan water. I watched it a second to see if it would sink.

One moment it was floating on its side, sort

of half sinking and half not sinking. The next moment, a huge splash erupted where the fish was. The whole creek surface seemed to rise in a bulge beneath it.

The splash flattened out, as splashes do. Then the water settled and resumed its smooth, dark flow.

The fish, that whole ten-inch fish, was gone.

22

We got home from the park at five. We took Lynn's bike helmet back and thanked her. Bethany had whined like a mosquito in an air race. Nothing suited her. She didn't like riding double on the bike because the bar hurt when she sat on it. She didn't like going to a park with no ducks. She didn't like the helmet. She wanted me to buy her a snack on the way home. She was thirsty. Gripe, gripe, gripe. What a cranky little kid.

I wasn't really listening to her, though. I was still dumbfounded.

What was that thing in the creek?

I was going to tell Lynn all about what I saw, but she was in a hurry—she and her parents were going out to a recital. So I had to go home without telling a soul. It half killed me.

Auntie Claire picked up the kids at 5:23. I had the table set at 5:25. I was hungry, yes. But far more important, I wanted that time when we sat around telling about our day while we ate. I could barely wait to tell the family about mine!

My sisters were surprisingly cheerful for having had the little darlings so long. After they told all about their woes, Hannah ended it by saying, "And just think! Only four more days, and it's over! They'll go home, and we can have a life again!"

So *that's* why they weren't as glum as Scrooge.

Then, at last, it was my turn. I could tell them all about our afternoon at Sugar Creek. I described the huge monster that grabbed the dead fish. I put in all the details, including how the water rose.

Dad stabbed at the lettuce on his salad plate. "Sometime when you're wandering through a physics book, check out why water lies flat."

"What do you mean?"

"I mean that, between gravity and surface tension, water doesn't make humps like that."

"But I saw it! It did!"

"I think you saw an optical illusion. That means a trick of the eye—or of the mind. It looked like a hump, but it wasn't. It was just stirred-up water."

I glanced at Mom. She was concentrating on her dinner in front of her.

I dropped my fork on my plate with a clank. I said to Mom, "You wouldn't believe me when I said I never hit Bethany. But I didn't." And I said to Dad, "And now you don't believe me when I tell you what I saw. But I *saw* it! I might as well make my living as a liar. It pays the same."

And I left the table. When you get mad like that, you get sent away from the table anyway. I was behaving just like Tyler, and I didn't care a bit. I stomped upstairs, furious.

I half expected Mom or Dad to come up after dinner and straighten me out. But they didn't. When Hannah and Catherine finished their kitchen chores, they came upstairs to Hannah's room, but they didn't knock on my door or anything.

Once by myself, I apologized to God. *I blew one of Your ten commandments—the honor your father and mother one. I'm sorry.* Sooner or later I'd apologize to Mom and Dad, too, but I couldn't do it just yet.

I logged onto the Net and hunted around a little, but I wasn't in the mood for research. I was killing time, waiting until 7:00 P.M.

That was when the other Creekers usually went on the Net. There were a couple different programs where you could "talk" to other people. I would type something into the left side of my computer screen, and it would appear on the right side of their screens. Then they would type an answer, and I'd get it on my screen. And so you'd talk back and forth that way. On some computers you could do it through a microphone. That was just like using a telephone. But most of us kids didn't have that kind of fancy equipment.

In fact, Mike didn't have a computer at all. He'd go next door to Tiny's house, and they'd log on together.

I opened with: SAW THE MONSTER TODAY
Tiny: WHERE
Me: SWAMP LOOP
Bits: WHAT DID YOU SEE

I typed a whole paragraph describing it. I waited and waited for the responses. What was taking them so long?

Tiny: REALLY LIKE A DOME—A HUMP

I wrote REALLY—NOT AN OPTICAL ILLUSION

I wasn't sure I spelled that right but thought it was close enough.

Tiny: WHEN

Me: 4:30

Bits: MEET TOMORROW

Me: SOMEBODY TELL LYNN—SHE'S GONE THIS EVE

Bits: BRING SPEARS

Tiny and Bits talked back and forth some more. I watched, but I didn't add anything. I was thinking. A homemade spear is about the only weapon of war you've got when you're eleven. But why did Bits say that? Did she know something I didn't? Or was it just that she was a cop's daughter and sort of naturally gravitated toward weapons of defense?

And I had a pretty good notion that if she was thinking we could spear something that big, she was badly mistaken.

The next morning, I was the first one to the picnic table at Sugar Creek Park. But then, I'll bet you already guessed that. And I had my spear with me.

Back around the start of summer, we five all got fascinated with the ancient Celts. There were a lot of things being written about them— how they hunted, what they ate. So we pretended we lived in a European forest with the Alps looming on the horizon instead of high-rise apartments. Irish elk instead of rabbits. Wolves instead of stray poodles. You get the idea. The interest in Celts didn't last long, but we still had the spears we made then—if you can say that a long stick with a point on one end is a spear.

As Lynn and Bits arrived, I lofted my spear. "Why?"

"Self-defense. Also . . ." Bits dumped her bike by the picnic table and sat down beside me. "Think about it. When I saw the monster, I was splashing around the edge of the creek, chasing crawdads."

"I thought we weren't going to do that. Chase stuff, I mean."

"I wanted to see if the crawdads were laying eggs yet. So I'm just splashing around and *whoosh!* There it was. Now you say that Bethany was splashing around the edge yesterday when this thing came."

"Yeah. She was hitting the water with a stick."

"See what attracts the monster?"

Splashing in the water.

Oh, wow! I'd never thought about that. What if that huge something had grabbed Bethany instead of the fish?

Tiny and Mike came rolling in. Tiny was really loaded. He had his binoculars around his neck, as just about always. And he had his nature daypack. It was like a school backpack, but he kept half a dozen field guides in it as well as a magnifying glass, pencil and paper, bug jar for collecting insects, and I don't know what else. And he had his spear, too.

Bits finished her thought. "So we use the spears for two purposes. One is to attract the monster, and the other is to protect ourselves if it comes after us."

"It's too big for a spear to be able to do much," I argued.

"Yes, but we have five spears." She smiled. "Five times as safe. So let's go get ourselves a monster."

23

In the bold tradition of the noble savage hunter, we sought the dangerous foe. Spears at the ready, we sloshed up and down the shoreline of Sugar Creek.

And we brave hunters also kept an eye out for the old lady in hiking boots. We were brave, but not that brave. Tackle a horrible monster? Sure. Stand up to a little old woman? I don't think so. All horrible monsters did was try to eat you. The lady was something else.

All up and down the creek, mostly above the Swamp Loop bridge, we found floating leaves and grass blades. Reeds and cattails were cut, too. They looked as if they were snipped right off.

Lynn looked intrigued. "It's as if the monster had scissors! Look how these are cut. Sheared right across." She held some blades of cattail in her hand.

Mike said, "The teeth on the thing must be amazing."

"I don't think I'd use the word 'amazing,'" Tiny said. "Try 'terrifying.' They must be sharp as knives."

A little later Mike pointed to a bare, muddy patch on the shore. "Here's some tracks. Are these raccoon or what?"

Tiny whipped a little animal-track hand-book out of his pack. They compared tracks. They counted toes. They studied. They leafed from page to page. In the end, neither Tiny nor Mike could say for sure what the animal was.

Just a little bit later, Tiny stopped us again. "Now here's something weird." He knelt beside the water.

It was kind of like a doormat, but there was no door. It was a flat little rug made out of mud and long, thin, cut sedge leaves.

"Do you suppose the monster made it?" Bits asked.

"What I want to know is why," said Tiny.

The Swamp Loop was named for—you guessed it—a swampy area. In fact, part of the trail was built as a wooden walkway. The board-walk kept you from getting your shoes soaked and also protected the fragile swamp.

"Maybe," Lynn suggested, "the creature moves out into the swamp. Like at night. Should we look for signs in the swamp?"

Good idea. So we left the creek and took the swamp trail. Part way across the boardwalk, we came upon a watersnake curled in the sun. It got very nervous to have five kids trooping toward it. With a flick of its forked tongue, it went over the side.

OK, I admit that the snake diverted us from our noble purpose. So did a big old turtle, which Tiny, from his field guide, identified as a map tur-tle. And the dragonflies there were amazing—

metal colored, crystal wings, and speed like a bullet. Small damselflies with black wings shared the swamp with huge bombers the size of your open hand.

"Look." Mike pointed to a raft of sticks, cut grass, and cattail leaves. It was a real raft, and it was floating. The soft breeze nudged it against a cluster of cattails, and we couldn't reach it.

Tiny studied it with his binoculars. "I can't see anything more than you guys can without glasses," he announced. "Maybe it's a grebe nest. They like to nest on rafts like that."

He saw a marsh wren in the cattails, but, much as I tried, I couldn't spot it.

"Hey," Tiny said, "did you guys hear the screech owl last night?"

"You have one in your neighborhood, too?" I asked. "So do we." And then we all talked about owls awhile.

We took the Swamp Loop to its far end, where it met the main trail again, and worked back toward our bikes along the stream shore.

"Oh no!" Lynn, the softhearted one of us, was the one who found the foot. It was a little rodent kind of foot with four long fingers and one tiny thumblike one. It probably had been some shade of gray when the animal was alive. We couldn't tell for certain, because it was so old the fur was slipping.

"It was sheared off," Lynn said, "Just like the cattails!"

So whatever our monster was, it was omnivorous. That means it ate anything it could lay its jaws on, plant or animal. We still probed the shore with our spears, but we stayed a little farther up the bank as we did it.

None of us had brought a lunch or snacks. So by noon we were all hungry, and we pretty much abandoned our quest. Playing around the creek was always neat, but starvation was a factor here. We started back along the trail toward our bikes.

"Duck!" Tiny barked.

I didn't ask questions. I ducked aside and flattened out behind a log. I didn't know where everyone else went.

We were actually pretty good at hiding in the woods. We sometimes played hide-and-seek the hard way—in the park. You could have three kids lurking within a rod (that's twenty feet) of home base, and you couldn't see them. You didn't dare go out looking for them, because three would sneak in behind you while you looked for one.

Then I heard the soft, sly sounds of someone walking by on the trail. There was a sort of tapping sound, too. Then the person passed, apparently unaware that he or she was walking right by five kids—five kids who were good woodsmen, I might add.

As the footsteps faded on up the trail, I listened for more people. None. So I raised my head slightly. I was pretty sure whom I'd see; there was only one person that Tiny would say "Duck" to avoid.

It was she, the lady in hiking boots. She

moved beyond the leaves and tree trunks. She disappeared.

I came out from behind my log. Mike emerged from the stump he had curled up behind. Where Bits had gotten to I had no idea, because she came walking back to the trail from streamside. Lynn had simply stood very straight and carefully behind a tree with a trunk big enough to hide her. Tall, lanky Tiny had run back the trail a short distance to find a hiding place big enough to cover him.

We continued on our way.

"Good call," said Bits. "I sure wouldn't want to deal with her today."

"Yeah," said Tiny. "Especially with spears in our hands. Can you imagine how her complaint would sound if she saw us armed?"

I looked at the crude point at the end of mine. "I doubt she'd recognize them as weapons."

Mike made a face. "She'd sure recognize *us*, though! We're the troublemakers."

She would, all right. I was glad we'd avoided her.

I was also very disappointed. We had seen a lot of great stuff. But what I really wanted to see was a monster!

24

Lunchtime was a little cool in our house. I knew it was because I was supposed to apologize to Mom and I hadn't yet. She knew it, and I knew it, and neither was saying anything. After lunch I took pity on the suffering sisters ("After today, just three more days!") and played dinosaurs with Tyler.

Say what you wish about monsters in Sugar Creek, his dinosaurs were real monsters. The artists who drew pictures in the corners of maps could not have designed more amazing ones.

Dad came home on time for supper. He seemed pretty happy, so I took it that his court case went well. He never talked about work, and I never asked, but his mood often depended on how well things were going at the office.

At dinner, I got to tell them about hunting monsters.

Hannah wrinkled her nose. "Did you find it?"

"No. Just signs."

"If you go after a monster and you don't find it, it's not news." And she launched into her horrible day.

When she paused for breath and a drink of milk, I asked, "So did you survive?"

"Barely."

"If you risked death but you survived, it's not news."

"Les, you are such a jerk." Then Hannah glanced guiltily at Mom. Calling people names at the table was a big no-no.

All Mom had to do was motion "Take a hike" with her thumb. With an exaggerated air of being put upon, Hannah carried her plate upstairs to finish eating dinner.

Then Dad announced, "I talked with Art and Jim today."

My ears pricked up. Those were Lynn's and Bits's dads.

"Are we still discussing monsters?" Catherine asked.

"Matter of fact, yes." Dad nodded. "So, Les, do you Creekers have a collecting permit?"

"To collect what?"

"A monster. The only thing you can legally take out of Sugar Creek without a permit is fish. And if you're a certain age, you need a license for that. If they catch you taking anything else, there's a whopping big fine."

"Really?" Suddenly I was kind of glad we didn't find anything.

"In fact, the three of us were talking about your monster," Dad continued. "Mr. Wing knows a limnologist at the university."

"What's that?"

"A scientist whose specialty is streams. Limnologists study stream ecology. That's a stream's geology—rocks and stuff—and everything that lives in it."

I was not impressed. "He'll just laugh at us."

"He is a she."

"Shes can laugh just as hard as hes."

"She has a collecting permit."

I was impressed.

"And," Dad finished, "she consented to go out to Sugar Creek Park with you after dark tomorrow night and see what's there."

"But the park's closed."

"To the public. Not to qualified researchers."

Qualified researchers. What a wonderful sound that made! A real professor of streams, who could tell us, if anyone could, what we had seen!

I was glad a fit of joy didn't get you booted away from the table like a fit of anger did, because I was almost jumping up and down.

Dad sobered. "Your mother and I value the truth, Les. We appreciate you for valuing it, also. This little trip up the creek tomorrow night is our way of apologizing for not believing you."

Apology accepted!

And then I managed to apologize, too— finally.

The next night at dusk, the five of us kids piled out of our van at the picnic area of Sugar Creek Park. Dad had picked up all the others at their houses so no one would be out on a bike after dark. Bits's dad had to work, but my dad and Mr. Wing were free. And with us came Dr. Carol Graham, limnologist.

She was a pleasant woman with brown, wavy hair, a happy smile, and a quiet personality very much like Lynn's. You didn't realize how much she knew until suddenly she'd wow you with something brainy.

We kids did not bring spears. We did bring flashlights, as requested. Dr. Graham put on chest waders. Those are rubber boots shaped like pants that go all the way up your legs and body to your armpits. She kept them up with bright yellow suspenders. She gave Bits and Tiny a seine, which is a big, heavy net with weights along the bottom. The rest of us carried jars, boxes, and notebooks.

The adults stood around, gearing up and talking, but I couldn't wait. I turned on my flashlight and headed for the woods. Tiny and Mike were right with me.

We hadn't gotten but a few feet into the shadows when a monster shrieked, right in front of us! I was so scared I couldn't move. I really could not. Mike turned and ran back. But Tiny was shining his light on the monster, and the monster was shining her light on us.

It was that woman in hiking boots!

"What are you little criminals doing here?" she roared.

"Boy, am I glad your dad's here!" Tiny exclaimed.

But I didn't want to hide behind my lawyer, so to speak. I hadn't done anything wrong. "All due respect, ma'am, you've made a false assumption. You think we're tearing the place up, but it's not us."

"Don't try to fool me! I saw the duck feathers on the water! And all the plants ripped out!"

By now, Mike had fetched the dads and the professor.

"Yes, ma'am," I said. "We found those signs, too. Ma'am, I'd like to introduce you to my father, William Walker, Dr. Art Wing, and Dr. Carol Graham, a university limnologist."

"I've heard much about you." Dad extended his hand.

She didn't seem to know what to do, so she shook hands with him. "Ruth Gardner."

And then I got an idea about the best way to change a false assumption. "Mrs. Gardner? We've seen a strange animal—a monster sort of thing—and we're looking for it. Why don't you come along with us?"

Tiny and Mike about turned inside out. Bits jabbed me in the ribs.

But Dad and Mr. Wing must have thought it was a good idea, because they instantly invited her, too.

Still looking confused and angry, Mrs. Gardner hemmed a moment and consented.

We were off to catch a monster for real this time.

25

I could see why Sugar Creek Park would be closed at night. This was just plain spooky. There were now nine of us, and still I felt scared.

That was ridiculous, because I was never scared when our family went camping. But . . . well . . . that's the way it was. The moon was no help, and even if it had been, the sky was becoming overcast. We didn't even have starlight.

We went directly to where Bits and I saw it, our favorite hangout on the Swamp Loop. Our special place, so cozy and pleasant during the day, felt ominous now. Black trees frowned blackly. The water slipped past us silently, darkly. Somewhere around the upper trail fork, a screech owl did its tremolo thing, chirring in the night.

Bits described how the monster looked as it came toward her. Mike pressed in close to Dad.

"Where were you exactly?" Dr. Graham asked.

So Bits stood right at the black water's edge, with no one able to see monsters coming in this darkness. That took immense courage. I really admired her.

Lynn told about the severed foot we'd found.

Then I explained what I saw.

Next, we walked upstream to where we found that strange doormat thing. Tiny could even find it again in the dark, using a snag as a landmark. On the way, he described all the cut leaves.

Dr. Graham knelt to look at the doormat. She stood up. "Anything in this area that looks like a beaver lodge?"

"It's a beaver?" I asked.

"No, I'm asking if you've seen a pile of sticks and leaves that's a rounded dome like a beaver lodge."

"There's that raft . . ." Bits suggested.

We walked out to the boardwalk and found the raft with our flashlights.

And on it sat a huge rat! Huge! It had heard us coming, of course. When we shined our flashlights on it, it dived into the water, disappearing instantly.

Dr. Graham smiled. "You children are splendid naturalists, very observant! You found a lot of signs and interpreted it wisely. I'm quite impressed. That raft is a feeding station made by a muskrat, and we just saw the muskrat on it. The cut leaves in the water are sure muskrat signs. And the mat you found, Tiny, is a scent post. The muskrat leaves its musk— its smell— on it for other muskrats to read."

"Uh-uh!" Bits shook her head. "What I saw wasn't a muskrat!"

"I think what you have here," the doctor

said, "is two 'monsters.' Let's go back to that first place."

"Oh, wow!" Mike whispered it, in awe.

As we returned to our special hangout, Mrs. Gardner kept crowing about never seeing a muskrat here before, and she'd been coming to the park often. In fact, she said, she was here tonight owling. The screech owls were about.

We gathered, all nine of us, on the bank of our favorite spot. It was so dark I couldn't see the log that the turtles bask on.

From the jar Bits carried, Dr. Graham got out some rotten meat. From the big steel ammo can that Dad carried, she took heavy wire fishing tackle. She put the rotten meat on a big hook. "Who wants to cast?"

Tiny got the OK. With a flick of his wrist, he put the baited hook in the water right where she told him to. He was right when he said he was a good fisherman. He reeled in slowly.

He did that two more times. And then I saw movement in our flashlight beams as the light played across the water surface.

"Again," the doctor whispered.

Tiny cast once more, and the monster struck!

It took Dad and Mr. Wing together to keep the monster from dragging the fishing pole away. Then Mrs. Gardner was in there helping them. Give the lady credit—she was enthusiastic and ready for anything.

As they dragged their catch toward the shore, it just got bigger and bigger and BIG-

GER. We kept our flashlights on it. The water domed up and rushed off it.

"It's a turtle!" Bits cried.

"I've never seen such a huge turtle!" Lynn exclaimed.

They took the words right out of my mouth. Its shell was over a yard across. It had three rows of tall, sharp ridges.

"This is amazing!" Dr. Graham said. "It's an alligator snapping turtle. There are a lot of common snapping turtles here, but we've never had an alligator snapper sighting in this area, and certainly never one this big. Art, you have the camera."

Mr. Wing took pictures of the turtle. He took pictures of us Creekers with the turtle.

Suddenly, with a wild, thrashing wrench, the turtle freed itself of the hook and slid back into the water. The creek ran dark and silent, with no hint of the monster in its depths. We all stared at the black nothing.

"It eats ducks?" Mrs. Gardner asked.

"Mostly fish, but it will take a bird, certainly. This one's big enough to do so—and to eat muskrats, too. That's probably the foot you found, Lynn. A muskrat victim."

Mrs. Gardner went on about how she never suspected snapping turtles, either. She even allowed as how maybe she'd been wrong about us Creekers.

But I was thinking. Knowledge, I figured, helps a lot when it comes to taking the mystery away, but it doesn't always take away all the monsters. Explorers erased the monsters around the edges of my maps, but the monsters in Sugar Creek were still there.

Dad's cell phone rang. He answered.

"What? Hannah, I can't understand you when you're so upset. Calm down. Control yourself! That's better."

"What's wrong?" I asked, instantly worried.

Dad was nodding. "Yes. It's all right, Hannah. It's all right. We'll be home soon. Yes, Hannah. Good-bye." He closed up his phone.

"What's wrong?" I grabbed his arm. "Is someone hurt?"

"Not yet." He smiled grimly. "But Auntie Claire got an extension on her research project. She wants the girls to baby-sit for two more weeks."

Other Sugar Creek Gang books:

Moody Press, a ministry of Moody Bible Institute, is designed for education, evangelization, and edification. If we may assist you in knowing more about Christ and the Christian life, please write us without obligation: Moody Press, c/o MLM, Chicago, Illinois 60610.